EDEN'S
HAMMER

BOOK III OF THE "DISTANT EDEN" SERIES

LLOYD TACKITT

CHAPTER 1

MARCH 2, MID DAY

H E ARRIVED IN THE VILLAGE with a crushing sense of foreboding gnawing at his gut. It had been eating him inside out the entire three weeks of the trip. Roman had called him home, saying they were facing a disaster, an event that could mean the death of everyone in the village. But Roman wouldn't say more over the radio. Adrian had to live with the open-ended statement until he returned home. It created such urgency that he pushed his horse as hard as possible to get home as fast as he could.

Roman gave Adrian a tight hug after Adrian dismounted. "Glad you made it back safely; we've got big trouble coming and need your help bad."

"Tell me."

"Big trouble headed this way," Roman repeated, momentarily losing his smile. "But there's time for you to rest up first. It's not coming today or tomorrow." With a strained grin, he added, "Those are nasty looking scars on your neck. Where'd you get that little wolf? And where in hell did you get that shitty haircut?"

Adrian smiled in spite of his three weeks of tension.

"Whoa, Uncle Roman! One thing at a time. The scars are from a grizzly bear I had a fight with last winter—they go all the way down to my stomach. I found the wolf pup on the way home, and I cut my hair with my knife a few weeks ago." He felt only a tiny easing of the tension. He had to know what the "trouble coming" was, he knew how fruitless it would be to rush Roman when he was in this mood, but he would try anyway.

"Now tell me what the problem is."

Roman reached a hand out to the puppy that was sitting on the horse's saddle where Adrian had been carrying him. It snarled and bit viciously at Roman's fingers. Snatching his hand back, he said, "Tough little guy, eh? What's his name?" The wolf cub continued a low rolling growl at Roman.

"Bear. I thought it kind of fitting, since everyone's been calling me 'Bear' lately. With a little luck, it might be confusing enough that the name will slide off me and stick to him. Tell me about the trouble."

"Not just yet. Not until I hear the story of you fathering grizzly bear cubs all over the mountains. I have to hear that one first. The ham radio net is buzzing with it. Did you really sleep with a grizzly sow?"

Adrian smiled ruefully. "That's a long story, better told sitting down. I'm hungry as a bear, though—when do we eat? Tell me about the trouble, damn it!"

Sarah heard Adrian's voice through the open cabin door and came running out to him, holding a bunched up portion of her long dress in one hand to keep from tripping on it. Her face was lit up with a huge smile at the sight of the beloved nephew that she and Roman had raised from an early age.

"Aunt Sarah! My God, you're more beautiful than

ever!" Adrian laughingly shouted. The sight of her momentarily raised his spirits. He picked her up off her feet as though she weighed nothing and whirled around in happy circles. Roman whooped loudly and shouted, "Sarah, did you know you raised this boy to go off and have bear cubs? You're the proud grandma of four-legged creatures covered with fur. Bet they look just like him, too!"

Sarah pulled back to better see Adrian's face, and while beaming at him, she said, "Better they look like him than you, or they'd be too ugly to catch their own food, old man."

Roman grinned, scratched his head, and said, "You have a valid point there, woman. When do we eat? The boy is hungry."

"As soon as Jerry and Shirley can get here. Food's already on the stove."

Adrian's face lit up with an even bigger smile "Yes, ma'am. I'll unsaddle this horse and rub him down. You mind if the pup comes in the house? He's pretty young, and I don't want to tie him up."

Sarah walked over to the horse, putting her hand out to the pup and then scratching it behind the ears. "Sweet little thing, isn't he? Sure, you can bring him in." She plucked the wolf cub off the saddle and carried him toward Jerry's house with her. Roman shouted at her retreating back, "Go ahead, old woman, take little Bear with you—I don't want him getting used to me handling him."

Adrian winked at Roman, who snorted and said, "It's because she's been cooking and her hands smell like food."

"Sure, Roman, whatever you say. When're you going

to tell me about the trouble?"

"Right after I hear about the bear loving. You go on in and I'll take care of the horse."

Adrian said, "Thanks! I'll take you up on that." He pulled the rifle from the scabbard, grabbed the saddle bags, and strode into the house, shouting "Damn, that smells good!"

———————

Adrian cleaned his plate of its third serving, leaned back, and said, "That's the best meal I've had since I left last year. Aunt Sarah, you are one hell of a cook! I'm so full, I could bust."

"Does that mean you don't want a slice of pie?"

"Pie? Oh Lord, you should've warned me to leave some room. No ma'am, I couldn't possibly right now. Well...maybe just one small piece."

Sarah got up from the table, returning with a large wedge of pecan pie. "Try this—it's not as sweet as I used to make it, but I think it's every bit as good anyway. Jerry and Shirley said they'd be here after you ate; they didn't want to eat me out of house and home by bringing their families with them."

Roman chimed in, "Damn straight it's as good—I like it even better. We've gotten civilized again since the grid crashed. Took us three years, but we're making steady progress. Planted sorghum last year and made molasses. Got sugar beets growing this year; soon we'll have real sugar again. "

Roman continued while Adrian was eating, "After the CME destroyed the electric grid, things were hard. Had to hide out in the brush from all the walking starving from the towns and cities. That lasted over six months. Then the war with Mad Jack—that professional wrestler west of here. Then it was back to square one, planting crops and living by the skin of our teeth while they grew. Then we had a hard winter that was helped a little by the food we had grown, which wasn't much the first year. Got down to our seed corn by spring. But we pulled through long enough to make a second crop, bigger than the first one. The village grew up around us real fast, too, becoming the central trading point for a long ways in any direction.

"Matthew's wood-gas devices really helped, letting us use tractors again. That was a giant leap forward, that was. It also let us use generators to gin up electricity, too, another tremendous help. We can weld, run refrigerators, use power tools, and it keeps the field hospital going." Roman went quiet, afraid he had re-ignited Adrian's grief. Sarah gave him a look that said he was a bumbling idiot.

Adrian noticed their expressions, paused eating, and looked at Roman and Sarah. "It's all right. I can think about Alice without going nuts, even talk about her. Go on, you were saying?"

"I'm glad to hear that, son. That was the hardest thing in the world, her dying like that, and with a baby in her." Roman paused a long time. "Still hard for me to talk about it, must be hell for you." He paused again briefly. "The hospital she set up that had to be burned because of that damn plague has been rebuilt, in a different spot of course. It's still the biggest draw for people for miles and miles around. But now we keep outposts manned at the trails way out of town. Anyone showing up with plague symptoms is turned away. Hate to do it, but we can't afford to help them and risk plague in the village. There were quite a few plague victims after you left. It slowed down a bit a few months back, but some still wander up. Lord only knows how many died from it over the past year. We hear of whole villages wiped out now and then. Something you have to be mindful of when travelling. That's one of the reasons I told you not to talk to anyone on your way home. You didn't, did you?

———————————

Adrian finished the pie wedge slowly. Roman thought he either really was full, or the talk of Alice had killed his appetite. Adrian said, "Didn't talk to a soul. I came in off-trail and didn't pass your outposts, either."

Roman continued, "Best anyone can figure, there are maybe fifteen million people left in the U.S. Course, there's no real census because there's no real government. We hear of broadcasts now and then from what's left of the government, but they're just folks that had government shelters to get into. They have no way to help anyone; probably they'll eat up their own supplies and hit the road begging any time now."

Adrian asked, "What about Fort Hood? What's the news there?"

"First tell me about the bear lovin'—I'm dying to hear the details."

Adrian told the story to Sarah and Roman; it wouldn't be the last time he had to tell it.

When he was finished, Roman was laughing and slapping his leg. Sarah, aghast at the story, interjected, "You men move into the living room. I've got to clean up, and then I have chores to tend to. Go on, now, you're in my way and you'll be jawing for hours."

The puppy followed Adrian into the other room. As they sat down again, Roman said, "Fort Hood—there's a study. First, they discharged all the men they couldn't feed, like you and your buddies, sent them off with some rations. Some, the ones with families, they set up with area farmers and ranchers to form communities. Those haven't worked out so well. Seems most of them broke down pretty quick. Too bad; sounded like a good idea. But mostly they had too many soldiers that couldn't adapt to farming life, or the farmers couldn't adapt to having so many strangers. Some of the farms worked, though."

"What about the post itself?" Adrian asked.

"Not good news, sorry to say. They overestimated how much food they'd stored. Not having the time or the skill to raise crops, they turned to taking food from local farmers around them. They didn't wipe them out, but they put them in severe hardship. Those farmers didn't much like being taxed at gunpoint, but there wasn't anything they could do about it, except hide food, which they did. That went on for a while, then the plague hit the soldiers—hit them hard. I hear tell they lost ninety percent of their people in a few months. Living close together and interacting every day did it to them. That, and there not being a cure, and sure as hell no vaccine to prevent anyone from getting it. Now they're down to a skeleton crew of what they were after the grid collapse, and that's a whisper of what they were before. No one really knows what the plague is or where it came from, but it seems to have started in Atlanta. The best theory I've heard is that some fools broke into the CDC and opened up a Pandora's box of diseases. Jennifer is running the hospital now and thinks that maybe some of the viruses mixed or mutated into something no one's seen before, says the symptoms aren't like anything she's ever heard of.

"We've been hearing rumors about the Navy in Corpus Christi. Word has it they've docked some nuclear powered air-craft carriers and subs down there, but haven't heard how many. If you can believe the rumors, they're pulling electrical power from the ships to a refinery and they're starting to make diesel and gasoline. Kind of makes sense—those boats should have been hardened for EMP attacks, especially the subs. Funny thing is, we never hear anything at all from the Navy itself on the ham radio, just stories about them. Seems like if it were true, the Navy would at least let us know they are there; it would be some small comfort to know part of the government still worked. Then again, maybe they don't want to be overrun by refugees, might already have all they can handle without beggars coming out of the woods, too. Hell, people might come from all over the States to get there."

Adrian said, "Neither you nor Sarah has said anything about the family, so I guess everyone is okay?"

"Sure, they're all doing fine and will be tickled to death you're home. They've missed you, we all have. Alice's death hit all of us hard. She was a wonderful person, had become Sarah's best friend in the world, or what's left of it, and that made it even more of a bond. We still miss her something awful, always will I guess. Sarah was especially tore up about the baby. She felt guilty for not telling you that Alice had told her she was pregnant; but it was Alice's wish to surprise you, and well, after Alice died Sarah thought if you didn't find out it would be for the best. She would have taken that secret to her grave, keeping it even from me in order to spare you that pain. She's a damn good woman, and that would have eaten on her for the rest of her life. I'm sorry you had to find out, but at the same time I'm relieved that she doesn't have to carry that.

"Speak of the devil. There they are now." Roman said.

Roman and Sarah's two children and their spouses—Jerry and his wife, Karen; and Shirley and her husband, Dave—came through the door, followed by their five children. Sarah came out of the kitchen to join in the homecoming. Adrian was happily surrounded by his cousins and nieces and nephews. Roman and Sarah had taken Adrian in after Adrian's parents had been killed in a car crash when he was eight years old, and this was his family.

Jerry and Shirley, officially his cousins, were more like brother and sister to him, having lived with them for ten years. Adrian was two years older than Jerry and four years older than Karen. They looked up to him as a big brother. Hugs, kisses, and backslapping took over the room. When everyone found a place to sit, Adrian had to recount the events of the year he had been gone. Because some of the children were still quite young, Adrian omitted some of the facts about his war with the cannibals. He would fill his cousins in on the details later. The children were thrilled by the bear stories, and two of the littlest girls clapped their hands in delight when Adrian described the bear cubs. The boys were all secretly planning to make spears the next day and go hunting.

When Adrian finished his story, there was a long,

comfortable silence. Adrian was soaking in his family's warmth and their obvious love for him. It was a good feeling, the best feeling he had had since before Alice's death. Finally, Adrian said, "I have to apologize to all of you for taking off like that; I know it wasn't right. Well, I know it now; I didn't then. At the time, I was hurting so bad that it was the only thing I could think to do, so I ran away and tried to hide in the mountains. Honestly, I wasn't planning on ever coming back. If it hadn't been for the circumstances I got into, I might have stayed hidden up there for years before I had enough sense to come back. I realize now that it was selfish to run off when all of you were hurting from her death, too. I can't apologize enough."

Shirley went to Adrian and gave him a big hug. With tears in her eyes, she said, "I know I speak for all of us when I say we know how much pain you were in. Alice was wonderful, we all loved her, and we all still miss her. There's not a day goes by that she isn't in our thoughts, and we talk of her often. The entire village loved her and still misses her. For you to lose the love of your life—and so soon after finding her—was devastating. Then to find out she was carrying your baby...well, no one here blames you a bit, or thinks any less of you for taking off."

Adrian looked around the room. There wasn't a dry eye in the house, and suddenly Shirley pulled him to his feet and everyone spontaneously gathered around for a family hug with him in the center. It was a delayed sharing of grief that staggered Adrian with its depth of emotion. He knew he had been a fool to run away from this much love and support, especially while they were hurting, too, and here he was, a year later, and they were sharing with him their love and understanding of his pain. Hot, scalding tears streamed down his face, and for the first time in his entire life, he wasn't embarrassed to be seen crying.

MARCH 2, NIGHT

Later, when everyone had gone home and Sarah had gone to bed, Adrian asked Roman, "What about my men? Are they all still here?"

"All five of them, and they're sound and healthy," Roman replied. "They'll be throwing you a party when they find out you're back. They've heard about the bear cubs, so I expect you'll get some heavy ribbing—not that you don't deserve it. I'll send the word to them after a bit."

Adrian asked, "How about you and Aunt Sarah? How have you two gotten along since I saw you last?"

"Pretty darned good, I'd say. We've had enough to eat, and good Lord willing, we'll have a record crop this year. Knock on wood that Mother Nature doesn't do something to it. This lifestyle has gotten me into better shape than I was in before the grid went down. Back then I sat at a desk all day, or was driving the hour and a half to work and then back. I was soft, really soft, but not now. Not an ounce of fat on me, and I can run like I was a child—well, almost that good. Sarah has leaned down, too, and she's always busy taking care of this place and me. She works hard. She's often in the field, weeding or harvesting. Chores that used to be easy, like washing clothes, take a lot more work and time now. I'd say she's in better shape now than she was in her twenties. Not bad for people in their mid-sixties; we're way healthier than we used to be. We're always busy and there is always work to be done, but we don't mind it because it's our work for our benefit. It takes hard work to survive, but every drop of sweat is for us, no taxes rob us of our hard work for the benefit of lazy people somewhere else. We share with others, but it's our choice what we share and who it goes to.

"All that prepping I had been doing in the grid years paid off. Those antique tools I collected have been lifesaving, literally. The guns and ammunition I collected have been worth their weight ten times over in what gold used to be worth. My library of survival books really did the trick for us in so many ways, it's hard to describe. The Foxfire books weren't especially helpful in the very beginning, when we were hiding and living by the skin of our teeth, but now that we are settling into a village lifestyle, they are precious beyond words."

Adrian said, "Now, tell me about this threat before I strangle you."

"Well, I can tell you a little. There's a lot we don't know, but what we do know is bad. There's a large band of raiders heading this way. Real barbarians— vicious. They're looting, killing, and raping as they come. It's a big band, don't know how many exactly, but from the accounts we've heard so far, it could be upwards of two hundred or more of them. Well armed and utterly ruthless. I've been plotting the reports of the raids we've heard about on a map and they are on a beeline right at us. One refugee even said that he overheard the raiders talking about Fort Brazos. That might not mean anything, but all information so far indicates they will be coming through here. Linda knows the most about them—I'll get her over here soon so you can ask her questions. Best guess is that we have five or six weeks before they're here."

CHAPTER 2

JANUARY 8

REX SHUDDERED INWARDLY WITH INTENSE pleasure as he watched the man thrashing out of the last of his life. Rex's outward appearance was of a handsome yet stone cold killer with no emotions; the wide, toothy smile on his face didn't signal anything recognizable as pleasure. He was a tall, blond man with pale gray eyes, almost albino looking. His face was always serenely still and cold. When he smiled, which he did frequently, it was a large, toothy smile that on an ordinary person would have been both charming and engaging, but on his face, paired with his dead eyes, it sent a primordial chill down one's spine.

Blood pumped from the man's throat, slowing quickly to a stop, pooling and sinking into the dry clay. Rex had few discipline problems with his men, but when he did, a lightning fast slash across the offender's throat with his large knife stopped the problem and made a crystal clear example for the other men. His discipline was so thorough that sometimes, such as in this instance, Rex had to create a perceived infraction so that he could release the tension that built up when he had gone too long without a kill.

Rex was asexual. He viewed sex as an unhygienic bit of business that entirely repulsed him. He'd tried it once in his teens, and then killed the girl afterwards in pure disgust, stabbing her repeatedly until he was exhausted. It had taken a lot of work to get rid of her body and not be a suspect in her disappearance. He'd buried her deep in swampland, where the corpse was never found. He'd also burned the motel down; there had been too much blood to clean up, and the fire had the added bonus of destroying any documents that might have led the police to him. As an added plus, the motel manager on duty that night went up in flames after Rex had knocked him unconscious. *On the bright side,* he thought, *that's where I learned to love arson.*

Lacking in normal sexual release, he found that his always-increasing inner tension was relieved by killing, at least temporarily. Killing was his sexual activity, and he was well aware of it. In fact, he reveled in it. Before the grid went down, his killings had had to be secretive, adding a layer of difficulty to his acts. Afterwards, when there was no law, he killed in the open and enjoyed it far more. He enjoyed an audience when he killed. The post-grid world couldn't fit him better if he had custom designed it. He was free to do whatever he was powerful and smart enough to do, and he loved it.

He was averse to getting any bodily fluids on him, except blood. He didn't mind blood, but would still quickly wash it off. Rex always took extra care with his appearance. He had two women captives that washed and ironed his clothes. He changed two, sometimes three times per day, washing himself thoroughly each time. One of the women trimmed his hair and shaved him every morning. They cooked his meals, performed the house cleaning and laundry, and shined his boots. Any tiny deviation from his infinitely detailed rules and routine, and the offending woman would receive a severe beating. Rex, ever aware of being poisoned by the women, even made them eat first while he watched. At random intervals, he ordered one of his men to eat his meal. He made it clear to the women that should they try to poison him, their fate would be hideous beyond their worst nightmares.

Rex had been discharged from the Army along with thousands of other soldiers at Fort Hood after the grid dropped, and the Army could no longer feed them all. He took his rifle, ammunition, and MREs and walked back to his hometown of Baton Rouge, leaving a trail of blood and bodies in his wake. He was born in Baton Rouge, and had grown up on the rough side of town. His first kill was at the age of eight. A slightly older and much larger bully had accosted him on the way to school. The bully was found stabbed to death a few days later. The police barely investigated, and certainly didn't think to look at children of Rex's age. Other bodies—mostly of the homeless—were found with their throats cut over the next ten years in and around his neighborhood. After Rex enlisted in the Army, Baton Rouge's unsolved homicide rate went down perceptibly. No one made the connection.

Rex joined the Army so that he could kill openly; he hated having to be sneaky about it. Killing for the good of the country, under orders, was still killing to him. It provided a cloak of acceptability that he found useful. He rapidly worked his way into a special operations unit.

He was large, heavily muscled, handsome, and fast. Even though he was outwardly an extremely attractive man, most women avoided him instinctively; the few that didn't, he brushed off as loathsome annoyances. His IQ was nearly off the charts, and he never hesitated to move aggressively. His combat skills and aggressive attitude outshone every soldier he was paired with, except one, and Rex had become overtly obsessed with besting that man. Killing him had become his constant inner drive. When the grid had dropped and the world changed for the better, his obsession had gone into hibernation, deep in the rotten swamps of his twisted mind. But it hadn't died. It laid in the darkness of his mind with one eye half open, waiting.

Rex looked at the body with contempt, then looked up at his men. He said, "There is only one penalty here. Be sure you're willing to pay the price before you break a rule." He stared the men down for thirty seconds. They avoided eye contact, knowing that any little thing could set him off if his bloodlust wasn't fully satisfied. Seeing no challenge from his men, Rex turned and strode back to his quarters, well aware of the cowed men watching him.

He had taken over one of the city's finest antebellum mansions. His office and personal quarters were on the top floor of the three-story home. His honor guard officers were quartered on the lower two floors. Rex's "office hours" consisted primarily of seeing a stream of informers. Men paid to bring information on the goings on of the city. Payment was generally made in canned goods, but sometimes it was made in favors, such as eliminating a particular thorn in an informant's side.

Rex had initially joined a small band of raiders

when he'd returned to his home city. Within a week, he had taken over the group by killing the leader in front of the men. He told them, "He was stupid and weak. Do what I tell you, and you'll be rich by comparison." The men believed he was telling them the truth. More importantly, he deeply scared them, and they fell in line immediately. He recruited more and better men until his crew had reached four hundred. It was the optimum size for the region's available resources. Once he reached the optimal level, he continued to recruit better-trained and more highly skilled men. When he brought in a new man, he would dismiss the worst man he had, maintaining his crew of exactly four hundred. During the initial weeks after taking over the original crew, they had taken food, water, and women from individual homes. When those resources became scarcer, and as his crew became larger and better trained, Rex upped the ante and changed his method of operation.

There were scores of gangs operating throughout Baton Rouge and the surrounding areas. Rex recognized these gangs as opportunities. Each gang, in order to survive, had accumulated food. Rex and his crew identified these groups, found their base locations, and moved in and took the loot, leaving just enough for the raided gang to survive. Rex didn't kill off the gangs; he let them accumulate more food and took it again. The amount of food gathered was greater than hitting individual houses, and required less overall effort, so it was a more efficient operation.

The trick was to locate where they had hidden the food—this is where the informers came in. The gangs were generally undisciplined and cowardly. Rex's men, by contrast, were superior in every way. Better armed, better trained, better fed and disciplined almost to a fault. Rex had trained the men similarly to the way he had been trained in the Army, instilling combat skills and discipline that he had learned in the far corners of the world. Theirs was a deadly army, quickly spreading fear throughout the region. He had a loyal cadre of forty hand-selected men, his honor guard. These were men that were given special positions and rewards and were rarely punished. They were his protection against rebellion from his troops. They were intensely loyal because of their privileges, and were uniformly feared by everyone. Rex sometimes took prisoners, occasionally recruiting the best of their lot while personally killing the rest. These were his substitute for sexual orgies, and he lusted for them as a satyr.

Rex had progressed to operating much like a rogue government. Citizens could come to him requesting favors or protection and Rex often complied, but only for a profit. He had recently begun thinking about rounding up women and prostituting them. Only his aversion to sexual matters had kept him from thinking of it sooner. They were a commodity that could be controlled and much profit made from. Another line he was working on was growing marijuana. Seeds were still frequently found, and he could use slave labor to grow and process the plants.

He already controlled the liquor market. He had recruited several men who were knowledgeable in the skill of moonshining and had them set up a distillery. Any competition he discovered was quickly crushed. His latest venture was growing crops. Food was the number one commodity on the planet. By taking over local farms and utilizing slave labor camps, he would soon be producing fresh food that he could sell at any price he demanded. Rex was creating an empire, and was evolving into an emperor. He would soon be recruiting more men, and there were plenty of men who would do whatever it took to eat. Rex's future was looking very bright, and he was enjoying himself more than he could have ever hoped to in the pre-grid failure world.

He walked up the two flights of stairs to his floor. It was shared only by the radio operator and a guard watching the operator. Rex had discovered the operator on one of the earlier raids on individual homes. The man had a top-notch ham radio setup. Instead of letting his men rape the women and killing all of the family as usual, he saw an opportunity. Rex had the equipment and the operator moved to the third story of the mansion. The equipment was set up under the operator's direction and the antenna was installed on the roof. The operator lived in a small bedroom with the equipment, typing reports on all the traffic he heard on an old manual typewriter. The operator's loyalty was assured by Rex's holding his family hostage in a nearby house. The operator's family was provided food and water and was kept under guard at all times. Occasionally, when the operator brought in especially interesting news, he was rewarded with a short visit with his loved ones. Rex had instructed the guard to ensure that the operator didn't make up stories in order to see his family.

JANUARY 15, AFTERNOON

Rex was relaxing in his office after granting audience to the usual stream of informers. At three o'clock in the afternoon, the operator brought in the day's dispatches. Rex took the typed paper from the operator and grunted, his way of dismissing the man. He settled back in his chair, putting his feet up on the desk, and began reading. There were the usual reports from around the world. Ham operators were an unusually resourceful and independent lot. Many of them had managed to scrounge up a source of electricity one way or another, usually using car batteries and inverters, and would go on the air briefly to announce and describe the local goings-on in their area. The stories were similar: mass starvation, and gang violence over food.

Third world countries had been the least affected by the huge coronal mass ejection as they had had little to no reliance on electricity before the grid went down, but raiding gangs still appeared as governments disappeared. From time to time, Rex would get news from his own area that was useful, so he kept the radio operation going around the clock. One report segment caused a stirring in his subconscious, something nasty started squirming deep in his mind. A man in Colorado was reportedly taking on a large cannibal raider gang single-handedly. Not only had he taken on the gang, but he was doing it with primitive weapons, and was apparently winning. Rex immediately wanted to know everything he could about this man. His subconscious was ringing a loud bell, and Rex never ignored those signals.

He quickly stood and went to the radio room. He told

the operator, "I want everything you can find out about this Colorado mountain man, every detail there is. Get your transmitter running and question the operators out there. Track down every rumor and story you can. Report to me in detail. You get enough information, and your family will get extra food and you can spend a night with them." He turned to the guard. "Vet everything—every report, every transmission, and the typed report." Rex walked out, not waiting for a reply.

Twenty-four hours later, the radio operator turned in a one-page typed report. The information was still sketchy, but one fact sent wild electricity surging through Rex's nerves: the mountain man's name— Adrian Hunter. Rex lost focus for several minutes while he absorbed the information. His obsession blinked and came out of hibernation with a roar.

JANUARY 16, AFTERNOON

Rex sent for the operator. "Double rations for your family for a week, and you can spend the rest of today and tonight with them. Show the guard how to operate the receiver and tell him to take notes on anything remotely related to this man, and anything else out of Colorado and Waco areas, too. Tomorrow morning, you'll resume. From now on, the only thing I want you to concentrate on is this. I want full reports every time you get more information. Otherwise, stay by the radio. Get enough information, and you'll get to spend more time with your family."

It took a full week for Rex to get a reasonable idea of what Adrian was doing. During that week, a plan was forming on how to find and finally finish off his obsession. He could return to empire building later, but until he fulfilled his obsession's demands, he knew he could never be content. Rex pulled out a road map that covered Louisiana and Texas. He had studied Adrian when they were at Fort Hood. Rex had fully intended to kill Adrian back then, but not quickly. He would torture him first, make him suffer as much as humanly possible. He had also considered torturing Adrian by killing his family before he killed Adrian himself. Using what information he could casually gather from listening to Adrian talk, he had learned that he had no parents or siblings and had been raised by an aunt and uncle. Adrian, unaware of the incredible depth of Rex's fixation, had not guarded his talk. It didn't take long for Rex to find out about where his aunt and uncle lived.

Rex marked the location on his map. They lived deep in the country north of Waco, on the banks of the Brazos River, so he didn't have a specific spot to mark, but he did have a general location within fifty miles. Drawing a circle around that area, he called in his best three scouts and sent them on a mission to locate the uncle and report back to him. "Find this man, but do not let him know he's being looked for. Do not approach him. Just find him and gather whatever information you can. I want to know if he is alive and exactly where he is. I want this information as fast as you can get there and back. Take motorcycles and fuel; ride day and night both ways. Do not attempt to use a radio to report. Do not talk to anyone whatsoever about this mission. This is top secret, and remains top secret after you get back. Do not leave anyone alive that you question. I expect you back in two weeks."

The three men saluted and left the room rapidly. They knew better than to ask questions or to come back without the information.

While waiting for the scouts to return, Rex thought through his overall plan, making changes, determining which men he would take and what equipment they would carry. He'd conceived of an approach that would motivate his men to move forward until it was too late for them to turn back. It also created a situation that would get Adrian back to his home in time for Rex to arrive and take him. Rex dreamed of how he would torture Adrian as he slowly removed his life. Rex had long planned how Adrian would suffer. He'd had a monstrously vicious plan before the grid had even dropped. The plan might still work, but if not, he could modify it to where it would be almost as good.

Smiling, he opened the small duffle bag of equipment he had previously gathered for Adrian and had brought with him back to Baton Rouge. He fondled every piece in the bag. The bag was small and tightly packed; he had kept it even though he hadn't really thought he would ever get to use it. Now, he knew its usefulness was back.

CHAPTER 3

MARCH 2, NIGHT

ADRIAN AND HIS FIVE FORMER squad mates—John, Bollinger, Isaac, Renny, and Clif—were sitting around an outdoor fire pit, sipping Roman's homemade whisky. Adrian said, "I don't know how he ages this so fast and gets such excellent flavor, but this would have been top shelf whisky in any place, and at any time. He did explain it to me once, but it was too technical to follow—sounded like a chemistry lesson."

Renny said, "You got that right. This stuff is hard to believe."

Adrian asked John, "So what's the story? When I left, you and Jennifer had taken over Mad Jack's place and were running it quite well. When did you move back?"

"We came back shortly after you left. Jennifer said she was needed here to take over the field hospital and run it. I had a choice: come back with her and be happy, or stay there with her and be unhappy, and you know the old saying: 'When mama's not happy, no one is.' To be honest, I wasn't enjoying being the top dog all that much. Mostly it was just a headache. Here, all

I have to do is take care of Jennifer and myself—way better all around."

"What about the rest of you guys? Ever thought of leaving and trying to get back to home?" Adrian asked.

Bollinger spoke. "We talked about it some in the beginning, but none of us thought it would do much good. We're all so far away from our original homes that it would take months of walking to get there, and what are the odds? All of us were city boys, and you know what happened in the cities. If we did get back there, we would have just about less than zero chances of finding any surviving family, and none of us had any close family to start with. Not having close kin was why we were all in that unit—or, at least, one of the main reasons." The other men nodded.

Isaac said, "This *is* home. It was home from the moment we walked out of that bamboo and Roman called us his sons. I'd never been called 'son' by anyone before, and he genuinely meant it—still does. I wouldn't leave here; it's home, Adrian, the home I never had. I'm married and happy and I do work I enjoy."

Clif, who rarely spoke, chimed in. "What would we go back to? An orphanage? Foster parents who only saw me as a meal ticket? No, I'm here and staying." Adrian was impressed by what, for Clif, was a long speech. Clif had been with Adrian the longest, had been on the most missions with him. There was a special bond between the two because of the years together and the dangers faced. He could always count on Clif to have his back and do what needed to be done. Adrian reflected, *"That's the most he's said at one time in years."*

Adrian replied, "You know, when I think back on it,

we were more like a family than a military unit. I think that's why Roman took to you guys so quickly. He sensed the bond we already had. Roman raised me as best I would let him after my parents died. He treated me exactly the same as he did his own children, loved me just as much. He's truly been like a second father to me".

Adrian shifted around to face the men more fully.

"Okay guys, we've apparently got some raiders headed this way. A bunch of them, maybe up to two hundred. We don't know enough about them yet. Getting good, solid information is absolutely essential. I'm going to be organizing a fighting unit here with the men from the village and surrounding area. My first thought was to put each of you in charge of a group. It makes sense because you have the most experience. But our first priority is intel. We need detailed, rock solid intel. I trust you guys to find the raiders, scope them out, and report back what needs to be known. I can't expect anyone else in the village to provide the in-depth quality or type of information that you guys would. You know what we need to know; anyone else would have to be trained and there isn't time for that.

"I also considered having you guys take over the fighting groups when we have the information we need, but there's a problem with that. I'll be training the fighting groups while the information is coming in. That means each group will have a leader, and they'll get used to that leader while training. Even though each of you would be ten times better at leading them, there would be a lack of that comfort the men get training together. You wouldn't have shared the training with them, wouldn't know what to expect from each individual, and they wouldn't know what to expect from you.

"So what I'm thinking is that initially, you men will do the scouting. When the scouting is done, I won't put you in charge of a group, I'll assign each of you to two groups—maybe three, depending on how many men I can round up. To keep the group leaders from becoming jealous or resentful of you being put in charge, I'm going to call you 'combat advisors.' I'll explain how we have been sent out on many missions to advise indigent combat groups, how we fought beside them and provided them with technical expertise without being in command. I believe this will prevent potential misunderstandings, and provide the best possible way of assisting them. In many ways, this really is just like those advisory missions we went on. I'll have the confidence of knowing you'll be in the thick of things, able to adjust the men to adapt as necessary to any given situation.

"What I don't want to do is cause any of you to wonder why you won't be given a military rank for this operation, or to feel slighted in any way. Everyone else will have rank—you guys won't—but it's you that I will be fully dependent on to bring this thing off. What do you think?"

"Bollinger, you tell him," Clif said. Adrian smiled; that was more like the Clif he knew.

Bollinger said, "Sounds like a good plan to me. It takes everything into account, and it's a smart move."

Adrian waited to see if there would be any more comments. There weren't. The men just looked steadily at him, waiting for orders. Adrian thought, *just like old times. God, I miss those days.*

Adrian finally spoke again. "Tomorrow, two of you will go out and get the information on what we're going to be dealing with. Any volunteers to be first?"

MARCH 3, MORNING

John and Isaac left before daybreak, promising to be back as quickly as possible—which was most likely in a few days—with the information. The other three were a little let down that they hadn't been the first to go, but they knew their turns would come soon enough. Waiting was a skill soldiers develop, so they waited the way soldiers usually waited: bitching and crabbing amongst themselves. A soldier that didn't bitch about a soldier's life was a soldier with low morale.

Adrian walked the village to get an idea of the new structures and people, reviewing the terrain and building placements for defensive purposes. Roman walked with him. As they passed yet another new cabin, Adrian said, "Looking at this place It's hard to believe I was only gone a year. It's three times bigger, and I see so many faces I don't recognize."

Roman replied, "It could have been ten times, maybe twenty times bigger, but we've been extremely picky who we let in on a permanent basis. There are still many just looking for an easier ride, people who would be anything but an asset. Some of the grid survivors are just plain loony, also. As it is, we've still grown too big too fast. What was a tribe is a small town now. We've gone from the original handful to over two hundred. It's unwieldy, but we let in people who have skills we need. I don't know which I am prouder to have here: the doctor or the shoemaker. It's unbelievable how fast we wear out shoes now, walking everywhere we go, working in the fields, going out hunting. We're going to have to change our setup soon, though. Tribal meetings don't work well anymore, and the majority of the villagers are new. The newcomers have been patient with me running things, but it can't last much longer. We need to be better organized."

Roman stopped and bent down to retie one of his shoe laces that had begun to come loose. He straightened up and resumed after a short pause, reminding himself of where he was in his talk.

"Thinking about that, I invited two new families in—old friends of mine. Perry was a lawyer, best one I ever knew, smart as hell and extraordinarily honest for any man, much less a lawyer. I asked him to come and write us a new constitution and a new set of laws. He's been here a bit over six months and says they are almost ready to publish. The proposed laws are written in plain language that anyone can understand, but that didn't make them easy to write. It's amazing how hard it is to write a simple declarative sentence that can't be twisted to suit anyone's needs, tortured into a meaning it was never intended to have. There's nothing more diabolical than the human mind when it is in trouble. But if anyone can do it, Perry can. He's borrowing a lot from the old Constitution, but he's plugging the holes in it. The new one won't be warped into what the old one was turned into. We're intent on Learning from our past mistakes, so that this one will be much clearer, simpler, and harder to ruin. Along with the constitution, he's writing an instruction manual on how to follow it, getting into more detail on the thought process and philosophy behind it and using concrete examples. It's sort of like the Federalist Papers, but his are officially binding because they are referred to in the constitution itself as such. Then the instructions refer back to the constitution, making a loop that's going to be damn hard to break. I'm looking forward to reading it from corner to corner when he's finished. It's a hell of an undertaking.

"When the new constitution and laws are published, they'll be distributed to each resident of voting age to study. By the way, voting age—at Perry's suggestion—has been set at sixteen. In this brave new world, you're an adult at sixteen, like it or not. A few years from now, we'll begin having elections as the first appointed office holder's age or die. I'm appointing the first office holders to make sure this gets off to a solid start, the way we want it to go."

"The new constitution will be the law; anyone who disagrees can pack up and leave—and damned fast, too. I started this village, and I intend to put into place a solid system before I let go control. Perry has also created a code of laws that is fair and simple. There will be only a few criminal laws; they are written in plain English, and they have teeth. There are three forms of punishment: community service or reparation, banishment, and death. We'll have no prisons or jails; however, in preparation for future growth down the generations, imprisonment is provided for, as well. Perry will be our judge, and all trials will be by peer jury. The jury sets the punishment if they find the person guilty. Perry's also working on a new set of contract laws, which, it turns out, is more complex. Those, too, will be in plain English—well, as simple as possible, given the intricacy of commerce—and will be impartial between trading partners. I don't expect to see those for a year or two, but they are codified into the new constitution by reference.

"The other old friend I was talking about is Tim. I asked him to come and be our town marshal, so to speak. We'll come up with a different name for it, I think, but his job will be to keep the peace on a day-to-day basis and bring charges against individuals as necessary. Indictments will be by a system similar to a grand jury. I asked Tim to come because he is extraordinarily level-headed and has integrity that people intuitively respond to. He'll be fair and he has no ties in the village, other than being an old friend of Matthew's, Perry's, and mine. By the way, Tim's hobby is long distance shooting. He has a fifty-caliber rifle that he can pick strawberries with at a half mile or more."

Adrian had only been partially listening to Roman. His focus was on keeping the village alive. Roman's plans for the future were good and necessary, but there was a higher priority on Adrian's mind at the moment. Adrian said, "This place is hopeless against a large band of determined raiders, Roman. We could give them hell for a day, maybe, but there are too many weak spots they could break through, and not near enough time to fortify those spots. Once this particular raider band is dealt with, we need to make those fortifications and then some. But for now, we're obviously going to have to take it to the enemy and keep them away from this place."

Roman just nodded. He understood what was driving Adrian's thoughts and wasn't the least bit put off by his long, rambling speech being ignored. He also knew Adrian well enough to know that he had absorbed the important parts of what Roman had said; the boy could absorb information like a sponge and store it for future reference while doing something else entirely. It was one of the many reasons he had wanted Adrian to come home. Adrian wouldn't be distracted from the mission of defeating the raiders by anything in Heaven or on Earth.

MARCH 3, MID MORNING

They arrived at Matthew's blacksmith shop and entered. Matthew was holding a sawed-off over-under shotgun that had been modified with a slide action from a pump shotgun.

Matthew shouted, "Adrian! You're a sore for sighted eyes! What got hold of you and where did you get that sorry haircut? Come over here and sit in the barber chair and let me fix that. On top of everything else, I'm the town barber now, too!"

After they shook with strong grips, Adrian asked, "Barber? How in the hell did you pick that trade up?"

"Aw, you know I've got two growing boys, and I was cutting their hair outside one day when someone walked by and asked how much I'd take for a haircut. Word spread, and next thing you know, I'm getting extra corn and bullets for something that simple. Cutting hair is easy. Sit down, I can't stand looking at you; it looks like rats have been nesting in your hair."

"I cut it myself with a bowie knife back in the mountains," Adrian said as he sat down in the barber chair.

"Yeah, that would explain it." Matthew started

snipping. "This'll only take a couple of minutes, and then maybe you'll stop scaring defenseless women and children."

Roman took a chair and watched with a smile. "There was a reason I brought you here this morning, Adrian," he said.

Adrian asked Matt, "What's that rig you were holding? Never saw an over under shotgun with a pump on it before."

"It's my newest invention. I just got it perfected, and I'm ready to give it a field trial. It's a wild boar gun. You know how hard those pigs are to kill? Well, this little beauty will stop them dead in their tracks. It's black powder and shoots a .779 caliber bullet that weighs a ton. It's a sabot round. The slug is bimetallic with a hardened iron center made of three flechettes surrounded by soft lead, giving it both deep penetration and wide expansion. "

Matthew adjusted the tilt of Adrian's head with finger pressure, then continued talking.

"It's fast loading because it's a breach loader—the rounds are placed in and the powder inserted behind it after breaking it open. The black power is a pre-measured quantity wrapped in wax paper. Once the powder is inserted, you tear a small hole in the end to expose the powder to the sparking device. I have a small piece of sharpened steel on a chain attached to the side of the action for tearing the paper. The paper-wrapped charge is sort of like the ones used during the Civil War, but loaded from the other end. This baby is fast loading, no ramrods, and extremely reliable. I went black powder because I've learned how to make it and it's renewable, as they used to say. Saves those precious tailor-made factory loads for more important things, and it will bring even more trade in for black powder and bullets."

Matthew adjusted Adrian's head in the other direction.

"The pump is actually an electric generator. Remember those old shake'em flashlights? Like that. The electric charge goes into two capacitors buried in the stock. I made the capacitors with foil and cardboard and wire. Then I covered the capacitors in melted plastic so they're watertight.

They should last for decades. Pump the slide action to charge the capacitors, one capacitor for each barrel. There's a switch to alternate the charging path for each barrel. When you pull one of the triggers, it releases the capacitor charge into a little sparking device I replaced the firing pin with, and *boom*! That big old heavy slug will go right through the thickest gristle of the biggest boar and penetrate deep, taking out their innards, making a big hole in the pig. Big hole, deep penetration, acres of internal damage, and ol pig drops in its tracks. I think I can convert one shotgun a week. It should be a good trade item."

Adrian asked, "Why the electric stuff?"

"Because I can't make mercury fulminate caps. This way, I don't need to. This has a tremendously faster lock time, too—almost instantaneous."

Adrian asked, "Shot it yet?

"Many times. Works great on the range now I'm going hunting and try it in the field. I shot it into a couple of pig carcasses to see how the round would penetrate and develop. It worked great, blew a hole all the way through. As the lead part expands, the steel flechettes keep going, but on diverging paths. I aided this by making the slug a hollow point, with the hole in the tip ending at the points of the steel flechettes. The holes coming out of the pig were from the flechettes—those babies do travel. The lead all stayed inside, blowing up everything in the chest cavity. I shot it at various distances, and it has a rainbow trajectory. It's not a long-range gun. Shoot it over fifty yards, and you have to really start elevating the barrel. I was hoping for some rain so I could try it out wet, but it should work just fine. I want to put it to the real test before I trade any off, so I'm going to douse it with water and shoot it on the range again and then go hunting."

"There you go—you look nearly human again," Matt said to Adrian proudly.

Adrian stood. While brushing himself off, he asked, "How's the family?"

"Outstanding! The boys are growing like weeds, and their mama's as sassy as ever. Those boys are smart. Homeschooling is definitely the way to go; education is just too important to trust a stranger with. You guys get going, now; I got to close up shop and get to the range and then into the woods with my new gun. Good seeing you, Adrian. By the way, when are we going after those raiders?"

"Soon. We need good intel first, and two scouts left this morning. Soon as we can make a solid plan and round up enough men, we'll be on our way."

"Count me in, son, I'll be there."

"Already did, Matt. I knew I couldn't keep you away if I tried. Not that I would want to, you understand."

Roman said, "Matt, how about you round up Tim and Perry and the three of you come over for dinner tonight? I'd like Adrian to get to know you guys better."

Matt smiled. "Done deal. See you around eight."

MARCH 3, NOON

As Roman and Adrian completed their tour of the village and headed back home, they encountered Linda and her young son, Scott. Roman said, "Linda! Just who I wanted to see. This is my nephew, Adrian; you've probably heard me mention him."

Adrian said, "Hello, Linda, Roman mentioned you last night, I'm happy to meet you." Adrian was a bit surprised Roman hadn't told him how pretty she was.

Linda replied, "Happy to meet you, too! Is it true you have baby bears all over the mountains? Just kidding; those rumors and stories about you are entertaining as all get out, though. Seems to be all anyone talks about sometimes."

Adrian was momentarily non-plussed and Roman jumped in with a grin. "Linda, how about you and Scott come over for dinner tonight? Sarah's making fried chicken, and it's going to be something special. I swear I think she killed half our chickens in honor of Adrian's homecoming. Plus, it will give Adrian a chance to pick your brains about those raiders. Matt, Tim, and Perry will be there, too. What do you say, can you make it?"

"Absolutely. We look forward to it," she replied.

CHAPTER 4

MARCH 3, EVENING

THAT EVENING, MATT, TIM, PERRY, Linda, Scott, Roman, Sarah, and Adrian were seated around the kitchen table.

Linda gently chided her son, "Scott, please slow down. I know it's a lot better than my cooking, but show some respect and don't shovel it in like that." Turning to Adrian, who was smiling at Scott in male camaraderie to help ease the boy's embarrassment, she asked, "Adrian, I heard a lot of wild stories about you over the past year—what's the true story?"

Adrian replied, "I left here after my wife died and headed for the mountains in Colorado. I took it on myself to live a stone age life, to keep my mind occupied as a distraction from grieving. That's a hard row to hoe, but it helped. Say, Roman, I forgot to ask—did those people from Palo Duro Canyon show up?"

"Sure did—nice folks. They're turning into good farmers. That redheaded boy is one hell of a hunter, too. Glad you sent them to us."

Adrian looked back at Linda. "When I got into the mountains, I got cross-ways with a group of cannibals.

They ticked me off some, so I decided to take them to school. I went to war with them, stone age style. That lasted for quite a while, with me slowly picking them off. But then they took hostages from a nearby village, so my war with them ended at that point. I went to the village and they were just about to launch a frontal attack on the cannibals."

Adrian paused to take a drink of water. "

The villagers would have gotten the hostages killed and lost most of their men, the way they were going about it. They asked me to lead them since they knew I'd already been fighting the cannibals and had military experience. Actually, I went there to ask them to help me, so it was a mutual thing. We finished the cannibals off in less than two days, but their leader got away. He was a vicious animal, called himself Wolfgang. Me and another fella went after him and got him a bit later."

Linda asked, "How many of them were there?"

"About eighty or so."

"And you actually took them all on single-handed?"

"Yeah, well, I got a little cranky, and it seemed like a good idea at the time. Having recently lost Alice and all, I wasn't exactly in my right mind. I'm not too proud of most of what I did to them, but on the other hand, they definitely had it coming."

Linda asked, "What about those scars and the story of sleeping with a grizzly bear?"

Adrian blushed just a bit; Linda liked that. Adrian said, "Not long after I got into the mountains, but before the war started, I came face to face with a grizzly bear. We had a fight and he clawed me a couple of times—that's where the scars come from. I finally got my spear into him and finished it. That meat fed me most of the winter."

Adrian pushed his chair back a little while Linda took a sip of water.

"During the war, I was grazed on the head by a bullet and got a bad concussion. The cannibals were hot on my trail and I was woozy, and getting worse by the minute. It was a dicey situation. I found a hole under a mat of tree roots that was out of sight. I crawled into it to hide and passed out. When I came to several days later, I was laying with my head against the rear end of a hibernating grizzly sow. I guess the smell of the bear grease I had rubbed on me earlier to avoid sunburn plus my bear robe's smell must have disguised my human odor enough to not awaken her. When I came to, I got out of there real fast, believe me.

"Later in the spring when we were chasing Wolfgang, we came across her and her cubs in the woods. She seemed to recognize me and left us alone, so I stupidly blurted out to my partner that that was the bear I had slept with. People being starved for good stories as they are, that one travelled fast. Too damn fast and too damn far—excuse my language, Scott. You know, it was the first thing Roman asked me about."

Linda replied while laughing, "Well, you've provided plenty of entertainment for a lot of people, nationwide. That's not a bad thing, you know. It's made you famous, too."

Adrian replied, "Yeah, but I don't much care to be famous for that."

Matt said, "You may not like it, but everyone else loves it!"

Tim and Perry laughed at Adrian's obvious discomfiture.

Adrian asked Linda, "What's your story? Roman tells me you probably know more about these raiders than anyone here."

Linda sighed and put her fork down. It was apparent that she did not like to talk about this, but with a serious expression, she replied, "A few weeks before the solar storm, Jeff, my husband, was diagnosed with pancreatic cancer. With modern medicine's finest efforts, there was a reasonable chance of him surviving it, but when the grid dropped, it was just a matter of time. After the grid collapsed, we moved out into the pine forest. We had a little place there that we'd planned to retire to and visited most weekends. We scraped by, like most folks, but Jeff got so weak that he couldn't help. He passed away a few weeks later. Scott and I stayed, and we were able to hunt enough to eat and had water nearby, had a good start on a garden. Scott is a great hunter, far better than you would expect from an eight-year-old. We would have eked out a living."

She paused for a long moment, looking lost in painful memories. Then she slowly continued.

"But then the raiders came. Some people who were fleeing ahead of them warned us, so we hid out and waited, hoping they would pass by. We were told they string out in a long thin line, living off whatever they can loot. Five men found our home, took everything we had left—which wasn't much—then burned the house down. They were just pure evil. They moved on; they could have left the house and we could have returned, but they burned us out, and destroyed the garden to boot. We slipped past them that night and kept going. We stayed ahead of them by moving pretty fast. They stopped a lot to steal and eat. I had hoped to eventually find a place far from them and start over, maybe finding an abandoned house in a good spot. It was a long, hard journey. We camped without fire, got soaked whenever it rained or we had to cross a creek or river, and caught what food we could on the run. It was the worst time in my life I can remember, aside from Jeff's death. We arrived here by accident, hadn't heard of it. We were quickly welcomed when Roman found out I was a farmer, so we stayed. It's a wonderful place and the people are so kind, but as luck would have it, the raiders now seem to be headed this way."

Roman jumped in, "Linda has a degree in agriculture. She looks at a field and sees soil chemistry, erosion patterns, crop rotations—things like that. Her family were farmers, so she has both backgrounds: real-life farming experience and a college degree. She's valuable to the village."

Scott had finished eating and asked to be excused. He left the table and Bear followed him. They went to play in the den.

Tim said, "The boy and that puppy sure have taken to each other. There's something about young boys and puppies that attract each other; must be that they're both in that playful stage of life."

Adrian said, "It's unusual—that wolf pup hasn't shown an inclination to stay near anyone except me since I found him. Linda, please remind Scott that Bear is a wild animal, not a domestic pet. If he plays too roughly with Bear, his natural instincts might flare up and Scott could get bitten pretty hard."

Linda replied, "I've already told him, and he listens

a lot more than you would think. If he gets bitten, it'll be a lesson he won't forget. He's a resourceful boy, bright and quick. He'll be okay."

Roman stood up, groaning from a full stomach. "Let's all go into the living room and talk. I've got some reserve whisky for you guys to try out."

Linda replied, "You men go ahead; I'm going to help Sarah and get in some girl talk."

Roman lit two lanterns, then retrieved a whisky bottle and passed it to Matt. "I've been aging this batch for a bit over a year, and it's good—some of my best yet."

Matt poured two fingers' worth into his glass and passed the bottle. After each had poured their own, Roman raised his glass in a toast. "Here's to good friends and good men, present and past." Each man raised his glass in salute and took a sip.

Perry said, "Damn, Roman, this is fantastic. How do you make it taste so good in such a short time?"

"Trade secret. But here's a hint: chipped wood. You're on your own from there, but that's a big hint. Adrian, these are the best three men I know. Between them, they more range of knowledge, expericnce, and downright contrariness than any three people on this planet. We're damn lucky to have them here. I wanted you to get to know them, because it is my firm belief that they will be of great value in this coming war with the raiders. They are resources you need to take full advantage of.

"Perry, as I already told you, is an attorney, and has more wiles and ways than you can imagine. Just ask anyone who has gone up against him in a courtroom. He never thinks inside the box—that would be too mundane for him. When you want to analyze someone else's moves, he's your man. His critical thinking skills are unparalleled. When you want to figure out how to outfox an opponent, he's the man to talk to.

"Matt you already know pretty well. What you may not know is that not only is he the village minister, blacksmith, inventor, and barber, but he has an analytical mind that can pick apart any problem, play with the pieces, and reassemble it the way it was or in whatever other form you might want. When you have to face a challenge of any kind that needs to be overcome, talk to him. He'll figure out the best approach and, if need be, build the apparatus to do it with. Matt was an engineer in the past.

"Tim was an engineer, too, and has extraordinary analytical skills. Tim has a way of cutting through the bullshit and getting right to the heart of a problem and then finding the simplest way to fix it. He has combat experience from Vietnam and he's a sniper extraordinaire. His combat experience plus his sniper skills are of inestimable value to us."

Adrian said, "So what do you guys make of this raider gang coming at us?"

Matt replied first. "Our information is sketchy, only what we've gotten from some refugees. We need more and better-detailed information. But from what we know right now, we have a serious problem. Either we take them on out in the field, or we wait and fight defensively. I've thought about making some pretty good anti-personnel cannons from pipe. Large muzzleloaders, so to speak. Load them with short sections of chain and fire into the raiders. They'll be effective, but limited in range and the number of times we could fire. They are slow to load, so instead, we would have to make a lot of them and make them portable enough that we could move them to where they are most needed at the last moment. When fully loaded, these cannons will weigh around a hundred pounds loaded. We could also make claymores and ground mines, but those might take more time than we have."

Perry said, "Matt's right, you know. We first have to determine whether our resources and abilities are better suited to offensive or defensive tactics. The two are worlds apart. That decision has to be made very soon in order for us to get prepared. If we wait too long to decide, then we've put ourselves into a no-win situation. Either way we go requires preparation and training and an organizational setup. One of the major problems we have is that we don't know how long we have to get ready, and preparation, training, and creating an organizational structure all take time. We have to decide on offense or defense and we have to do it fast; there won't be time to change strategy, and we can't do both and do them well."

Jim stood up and walked around the room while he spoke. "It's simple, guys. We have to attack them in the field as soon and as far away as possible while we take whatever defensive measures we can. It won't be fucking rocket science fighting them out there; it will be who shoots the best and has the most determination to win. We need to get every available man, do rudimentary training, and then go out there and just fucking kill the sorry bastards. We need to do simple training—nothing complicated. Make sure everyone can shoot straight, practice cover and advance technique, and set up communications. Communications among the men is a prime necessity, and has to be fast and accurate.

Runners are the best way to do that. We don't have enough field radios and we won't really need them; the battlefield will be compact, given the numbers we're talking about here. Let's keep it as simple as we can and get moving fast."

Roman said, "Adrian, my suggestion is that we call the village together tomorrow. I'll start the process tonight to gather them tomorrow. What I'll do is introduce them to you and have them vote on whether or not they will follow you into battle or not. I'm sure they will; they've all heard the stories that came out of Colorado about how you organized and led that village into battle with only a few hours to prepare. Many of them remember the Mad Jack battle. I'll also explain your military background and the need for quick organization and training. I'm assuming that you are willing to take on a leadership role, of course. Are you?"

Adrian looked at each man for a few seconds before replying. "I'm willing if you four think I'm the right person for it. You know the village men and their capabilities better than I do. If you're sure there isn't a better candidate, then I'll do it. If there is a better candidate—and personally, I believe I am looking at four better candidates—then I'll follow him."

Perry replied, "My opinion is that you are the best man for the job. There are two reasons. First is that you are much younger and far more physically fit than any of us, and this job is going to require long, hard work with little sleep. You have the advantage over us there. Second—and maybe more importantly—you have recently led men into battle in a somewhat similar situation, and the villagers know it. Your adventures have afforded you a certain charisma and people already want to follow you. Their being willing to follow is of paramount importance in their motivation to fight."

Adrian replied, "All right, then, let's see what the villagers say tomorrow."

Sarah and Linda cleared the table and were washing the dishes after the men had gone into the living room.

Linda said, "That was the best meal I've eaten since before the grid collapsed. Fried chicken is one of my favorites, and you cooked it perfectly. I want to thank you again for inviting us."

Sarah replied, "Think nothing of it, it's my treat to have you here. I can't remember the last time I had the pleasure of the company of another woman in the kitchen—not since Alice died, anyway. You're welcome anytime, no need to wait for an invitation. Just come on over whenever you feel like it, and if you time it to be here for dinner, so much the better."

Linda asked, "What happened to Alice? If that isn't too personal of a question."

Sarah gave Linda a knowing look and Linda's face turned pink. Sarah smiled at that and said, "Not at all, honey. Alice was a great friend, and, as you know, Adrian's wife. She was a doctor—a surgeon, actually. She and Jennifer and the nurses set up a hospital here. One day when she was working alone, a man with the plague showed up and asked for help. Alice immediately quarantined the hospital. Wouldn't allow anyone to come near, especially Adrian. She was a bit over three months pregnant at the time, but Adrian didn't know—she was waiting to surprise him. She told me, but made me promise to keep it a secret until after she told Adrian.

"Adrian sat outside the hospital, as close as Alice would let him—which wasn't close at all—until she died. They talked a lot across the distance between them, but she never told him she was pregnant. It was too late to tell him then; if she had, he would have come into the hospital no matter what and died with her, and she knew it. She had to threaten to kill herself if he tried to come closer, as it was. After she passed away, he burned the hospital down with her in it. Those were her instructions to get rid of the plague virus. When the ashes cooled, Adrian went in to get what was left of her for burial. Some ceiling and insulation had fallen across her stomach during the fire. Adrian found some tiny cartilage fragments that hadn't completely burned and figured out that she had been pregnant. Adrian loved Alice something fierce, and they had only been married a year, still in the honeymoon stage. He went a little insane and left only minutes after the funeral was over. But he seems to be over the craziness now. He's still carrying a lot of hurt, though—a whole lot of hurt."

Linda said, "Poor man. Hard enough to lose your wife, but to lose a child you didn't know you were going to have—that's beyond painful. I don't wonder he went a little crazy. When I lost Jeff, I had time to see it coming, and Scott to go on for. It was damned hard and painful. I can only imagine what he felt."

Sarah replied, "I know. That whole 'stone age living' thing shows how bad it was. That kind of desperation breaks my heart to think about. I loved Alice; she was a wonderful person. She died bravely, and well. That's about the best thing I can say about the situation. They would have had such a wonderful life together." Sarah's eyes had gone watery.

Linda said, "Here now, let me finish these dishes, you sit down and talk to me while I do it." She gave Sarah a hug.

The men in the living room had stopped talking for a few moments to consider all that had been said and what lay before them.

Scott asked Adrian, "Where did you find Bear, sir?"

Adrian replied, "I found him on my way home from the mountains. I was riding along and spotted a dead wolf, and Bear was sitting beside her. It looked like he had been there several days and was starving to death. I couldn't just leave him there, not with him being that loyal to his mother. So I decided to raise him up enough to be able to take care of himself and then let him decide what to do—go back to being wild or stay with me."

Scott asked, "He just let you pick him up?"

"Oh no. He put up a ferocious fight. Bit me several times. But I finally got hold of him and carried him across the saddle. I gave him some water and some meat. He bit me every time I moved him for the first couple of days, then settled for growling at me. Much as I hated to do it, I had to tie him up at night so he wouldn't wander off while I slept. Every morning, he would fight me all over again. Eventually he quit fighting me—mostly because of the food and water, I guess. He's growing fast, getting more food than he normally would in the wild. He eats all the time, eats like he's never had food before. He's smart, too. I haven't tried to train him, but he watches and listens and learns fast. It's only been a little while since I quit tying him up. I expect to find him gone some morning, but so far, he's sticking around."

CHAPTER 5

MARCH 8, MORNING

JOHN AND ISAAC HAD RETURNED from their scouting mission and gone straight to Roman's house to find Adrian. John said "We found them with no problem at all. You want a full briefing right now?"

Adrian replied, "How far out are they?"

"I give it three weeks before they're here."

"All right, then, save the full briefing until we can all hear it at the same time—it'll save you from repeating it. I have a few key men who I want to hear your report. I've been talking to the village men, sending out runners to recruit more. As soon as you've reported, we're going to send out two more scouts, then every three days, we'll send out two more to replace them and the two that come back will fill in more details. That way, we can keep a running eye on them and stay current. As the raiders get closer and the scouts have less distance to travel, we'll up that to daily reports by having two in sight of the raiders and one being replaced each day. Did you encounter any problems?"

Isaac replied, "No problems. They were easy to find and to watch. They're not trying to hide, and they leave nothing but devastation behind them. There are people running from them; you'll probably be seeing some more of those before long. Might get some recruits from them, too."

Adrian said, "All right, you two go on home and eat and rest. I'll spread the word to meet up here again at noon. Roman, would you ask Sarah if she can fix enough lunch for us?"

"Sure, no problem," Roman said. "I'll tell her to put the tea on."

"Tea? You have tea?" Adrian asked.

"Oh yeah, we have tea. After you left, we made several scavenging trips into Waco. We came across the arboretum and I took a look to see if there were any plants still alive that we could use. Found a few; among them were some tea plants. They grow well here and are easy to process. So we have tea. Not as good as coffee, but better than nothing."

Adrian replied, "Isn't that something. What else did you find?"

"You saw the banana trees—we got them there, too. I think we'll be able to harvest some this year."

"I thought those were ornamentals. I thought they froze here in the winter."

"They do, normally. But I read that if you surround them with a cage stuffed with straw heaped high over them during the winter, they won't freeze unless it gets a lot colder than it normally does here. In the spring, you remove the straw, and if they didn't freeze, they'll produce fruit. It's an experiment, but if it works, the kids'll love it. You'll also be pleased to know that we have ice. During the winter, we tried freezing water and then saving it inside insulated boxes, but it didn't work too well. Matthew rigged up an icemaker that's run off a portable electric generator that's run off a wood gas generator. Comes in real handy, and is also a nice luxury."

Adrian replied, "You have ice and didn't bring any out last night when we were drinking whisky? Ice would have been great with that whisky."

"Son, if you insult my whisky by putting ice in it, I'll never let you have another drop."

Adrian said, "Oops! My mistake." He grinned as Roman turned and stalked off.

MARCH 8, NOON

As the men ate smoked ham and cornbread and drank iced tea, John gave his report.

"We estimate one hundred and eighty of them strung out in a wide line. From end to end they're strung out for about a mile, although it expands and contracts, depending on terrain and resources. They're armed to the teeth, mostly military grade stuff. A lot of M4s, some AKs—stuff like that. Didn't see anything heavy, no belt feds or field pieces. Looked like they have ammo problems, though. Most of them carry two rifles, one military style. The other is the one they use most; they appear to be hunting rifles in a variety of calibers. Likely scavenged weapons that they can scrounge ammunition for as they go. My guess is that they save the military weapons for the rare cases where they encounter heavy resistance, but most of the resistance they run into is scattered families with not much to fight with, so they use the hunting rifles on them, saving their military stuff.

"They're dressed non-military, wearing an assortment of civilian clothing, but move with some discipline. Not a lot of discipline, but enough to make you wonder if they haven't had some training. They carry packs and have basic camping equipment. Tents, sleeping bags, ground sheets—that sort of thing. After they take over a house, they might stay in it one night, then burn it and move on. Or they might burn it right away once they've scavenged all they can. Depends on time of day more than anything. They all wear hiking boot-style footwear.

"Didn't see any signs that they are into personal hygiene; they had opportunities to bathe on several occasions, but didn't. I did see a few that took some care with changing socks and cleaning their feet, so I'm thinking there are some ex-infantry scattered among them. But from the looks of those few, they weren't good at being military. More like they absorbed some of the training, but not a lot of it. Overall, they are one hundred percent male, a mixture of races, mostly in their mid-twenties, and in good physical condition.

"It looks like a Darwinist kind of operation. With that many men, you would expect to see a few injured or sickly looking, but we didn't. My hunch is that if you're a member of that group and get hurt or sick, you get left behind, or maybe worse. We didn't see any left behind, so that's only a guess. But then, we didn't see any get hurt, either.

"Food-wise, they don't spend time hunting. If they scare up a pig or deer, they'll shoot it, but they don't go looking for them. Mostly, they're eating what they take from others. Food is shared fairly evenly among them, so they aren't raiding on an individual basis. A lot of them are wearing a bunch of rings and watches, kind of reminds me of pirates. There are a lot of tattoos on display, a lot more than normal people would have, kind of like what you see with biker gangs. Some of the tattoos are prison-style. Lots of spider webbed elbows. All in all, a pretty rough crowd."

"Good observations," Adrian said. "What about tactics?"

Isaac replied, "They have an interesting setup. They operate in groups ranging anywhere from six to ten men. Each group acts in a semi-autonomous way, but they are linked to a central command. Each group has a definite leader and also a second in command. After that, they appear to be of equal rank. There aren't any saluting or obvious signs of who is in command, but if you watch a group long enough, you can tell who's in charge. The second level guy is a bit tougher to figure out, but again, if you watch long enough, you can eventually figure out who he is.

"Each group operates independently, except for two scenarios. If a group encounters heavier than the normal light resistance, a second group moves over to help. We didn't see that but once. I would assume that if the resistance were heavy enough, the entire line would pull in to help. The other scenario is if one group finds more food than it can use, then more groups come over to share the wealth. In other words, they share risk and reward as occasion calls for it.

"Their standard procedure is to have scouts out ahead looking for likely targets. When a target is spotted one remains to watch while another goes back and alerts the group. The group approaches rapidly but covertly. They confer with the watcher scout who gives them the info he gathered. Then they typically divide into three groups and attack with all hands on deck coming in from three directions. They clear the house of occupants, then loot the house for food and weapons. They search the surrounding area for hidden food, sometimes finding some. When they leave they destroy everything.

"Communications between groups and central command is by runner. They have a constant stream of runners moving up and down the line. That duty appears to be taken in turn by each man in each group, but the central command has four or five runners that do nothing else. It's simple and effective, if somewhat slow. I get the feeling that the groups at the far ends are the most trusted by central command. Being the furthest out, that makes sense from a tactical point of view.

"The central commander isn't in the center as you might suppose. He moves up and down the line, checking on groups, picking up food and supplies and apparently keeping the line in order. That group doesn't take on raids, but frequently shows up when one has been completed. They are a lot more mobile, the men in that group seem to be younger and fitter. There's no doubt of their elite status, the regular groups show deference, extreme deference, the kind that's inspired by fear.

"We witnessed one disciplinary action by the command group. I don't know what the man did, but he was summarily executed by the central commander. One minute the commander was talking to the guy and the next minute the commander killed him with a knife slash across the throat. His body was left where it fell. We were too far away to get real details. The commander is big, but with the hat and sunglasses we couldn't tell much about him."

John continued, "When we left, they were a little east of Corsicana, loosely following Highway 31. When they hit small towns, they condense their lines and scour the towns, but it doesn't slow them down much because they don't find much. Then they spread back out. Their forward progress is erratic, given the way they operate, but it is a fairly steady five to ten miles per day. Call it eight miles per day on average. That puts them about sixty miles away as the crow flies, and they pretty much travel as the crow flies. I'd say they'll spend a couple of days in Corsicana, maybe two or three more days as they come across the small towns. Best guess is they will be here in three weeks, two at the earliest and maybe four at the outside. That's if they stay on the same track they're on now. They didn't deviate from it while we watched, though."

Adrian said, "Outstanding reports. We'll need two more scouts to leave right away. Bollinger and Renny— how about it?"

They smiled and nodded. Adrian said, "Actually, since they could be here that soon, let's make it three scouts. Each day, one of you will return and report, and another will leave from here. That will keep one scout watching, one traveling, and one reporting, so that we get information every other day. Clif, can you follow them day after tomorrow?" Clif nodded his assent.

"Good," Adrian said. "Before you men leave, let's talk about this some. First, any questions for the scout report?"

Tim asked, "John, was the central commander easy

to locate? Is he vulnerable to a sniper?"

John replied, "He's pretty hard to find, unless you wait where they'll come across a house. He'll sometimes show up there afterwards. He could be sniped if the terrain was right and the conditions were right. But he tends to stay in heavy cover, or have men all around him blocking. I thought about that as I watched him; his actions indicate he's given snipers some thought. It could be done, but the sniper might also spend a lot of time waiting for one small opportunity that never comes. Overall, I'd say it's a low percentage mission."

Perry asked, "There's no particular indication he is coming here specifically, is there? I mean, if you look at a map and scale out their line, the odds of them actually coming right here aren't huge, unless they are coming here specifically. So you have to wonder if there's a specific reason for them to come here, or if they'll veer off and miss us."

Roman said, "We've talked about that a lot, and going by what we do know of where they've been and the way they are heading, I think they are coming this way for a purpose. They haven't veered off a straight line toward us since we first heard of them. One refugee that came through indicated they've heard of us, probably because we do so much trade and have a hospital. Face facts: we've been advertising our presence by trading with anyone that has something to trade, and word of the hospital has spread far and wide. It's possible—even likely—that they've heard of us and got it in their heads that we are a prize worth taking. Fact is, they're right; we are a prize. We have a great setup, we're growing more food than anyone we know of, and we have medical facilities. Look at us—we're drinking ice tea; what do you want to bet we're the only people in Texas doing that? I think they are coming here specifically."

Perry replied, "Right or wrong, they appear to be coming here, and if they are, they'll be here too soon to hope they won't. They no doubt interrogate as many victims as they can, and the closer they get, the more they'll hear and know about us. So even if they hadn't decided on coming here from the beginning, odds are they will soon."

CHAPTER 6

JANUARY 18, EARLY AFTERNOON

REX WAS PUTTING HIS PLAN in motion today. The scouts had returned. Roman was not only alive, but thriving. He had developed a village complete with a hospital. Rex was thrilled to hear of the hospital; that meant his original plan for Adrian could be implemented without change. It was now just a matter of drawing Adrian back to the village and capturing him. He chose one hundred and seventy-five men for this operation. It would take weeks for the plan to develop. He assembled his chosen troops after informing the men that were not chosen they were to maintain operations until his return.

"Men," he said, "I have located a veritable Garden of Eden. A place where fresh food is plentiful, water is abundant, and warm houses await. There are plenty of women to amuse you and a fully equipped hospital for those times you may need one. It's a center of trade, and we'll charge outrageously for medical care. We will capture the village, make the men slaves to work the fields, and live like kings." The men cheered, an uncharacteristic action for them. For men who lived by raiding, this sounded like a dream come true.

"All we have to do is march cross-country until we reach this paradise, then take it for ourselves. The men there don't know how to fight; they'll be easy pickings for you. On the way, we will live off the land, raiding as we go. We'll travel light, but not too quickly. It'll be an easy march, but a long one. Pack your supplies and be here in one hour. Bring canteens, food, sleeping gear, your best hiking boots, and, of course, your rifles and ammunition."

Rex assembled his honor guard. "Men, I'll be gone a couple of months. Roger, I'm leaving you in command. All I want you to do is maintain operations as they are; you're not to try to expand or get into new ventures. Understood?"

"Yes, sir!"

By that evening, Rex and his expeditionary force had walked single file for most of the day. When they reached their first camping spot and the men had set up for the night, Rex called in his officers. "We're going to continue this course until we reach Fort Brazos. Don't worry, it's not really a fort—they just call it that. It's a soft village ripe for the picking. We'll spread out in a line about a mile across and pick up food and supplies from all of the homes and towns we come across as we go. Organization will be teams of ten men or less. Each of you will be responsible for four teams. Pick your four team leaders and their second in command carefully. Communication will be by runner. The runners will move back and forth along the line. Each night, we'll camp in the same order, teams spread out. I'll give you further orders as we go. Be ready to move out at daylight."

Rex dismissed the men and returned to his wall tent. He had chosen a camouflaged baker-style tent. Each evening when his men set up the tent, camouflage netting was placed over it and brush worked into the net. From a distance it would be invisible, the netting also allowing him to have a small, dim light inside without showing through the tent walls. Inside, the radio operator had set up the receiver and batteries that had been carried by the lowest rank men. A temporary antenna had been installed in a nearby tree. The radio was up and running. Rex had told the operator, "Focus on the Colorado and Fort Brazos signals. I want to know all traffic that moves between them. When I get the information I want, I'll send you and the equipment back to your family." He now stretched out on his bunk, staring at the tent's ceiling with unblinking eyes, seeing only images of Adrian suffering.

JANUARY 21, EARLY MORNING

Rex watched as the men began moving into a north-south line. They were heading west by north with four hundred and fifty miles of country to cross. Some of this land would be either swamp or pine forest until they reached the Trinity River in Texas. After that, it would be rolling plains. They would use roads only where necessary to cross difficult terrain. Rex wanted the men spread out to make as much "noise" as possible. His orders to burn every house along the way had been supplemented with another order: to allow some of the women and children to escape. He didn't explain that order to his men, knowing they would wonder but obey—after the women had been thoroughly raped, of course. He hadn't forbidden that. Rex wanted the news of his men's travel to spread far and wide and fast. When the time was right, he would step up his plan by planting the idea that the raiders were coming toward Fort Brazos, but not why. Using runners, he would keep the men in line in fairly good order.

By midafternoon, Rex could see plumes of smoke on both sides of his position as his men torched every building they came to. Burning the houses not only signaled their position, but also let everyone in the area know in which direction they were moving. It would take a few days, maybe even a couple of weeks, but it would soon be common knowledge. He had considered that other villages or small towns might send out men to attack, to stop them from reaching their villages and homes. He wasn't expecting any serious resistance, but if any were encountered, he would simply move around it and continue his line. His goal was Fort Brazos, not the people in between.

They marched all that day, picking up less food than Rex had expected. They were primarily coming across single farms and ranches with one or two defenders at most. He hadn't realized how poor the pickings out here were. These people were growing and raising their own food, not dependent on outside help, but having a hard time of it. Their independence and self-sufficiency was less than he had expected. His men were still happy with the results; they might not get fat until they reached his promised Shangri-La, but they were getting enough. *Good, that'll keep them moving forward until it's too late to turn back*, he thought. Once they were into the far side of East Texas, the pickings would be even slimmer as the farms became farther apart, making Fort Brazos all the more desirable to them.

They had been on the move for a little over a week, leaving death and destruction behind. Rex was continuing the scorched earth policy while allowing enough survivors to escape to make sure everyone knew about their line of march. The radio reports had been infrequent, but from the ones they had, he gathered that Adrian was still at war with the cannibals. He couldn't recharge the car batteries, but they were picking up plenty of them as they went. Every night before Rex went to sleep, he said what almost amounted to a prayer: "Please don't let Adrian get killed." Rex's plans would be ruined if that happened.

Rex visited a different group every night. He observed the men's morale and found it typically good. These men were doing what they liked best: raping and pillaging and destroying. The body count they were leaving behind had crossed two hundred. Rex made sure his men counted the dead—he wanted to know how many every day. Rex himself had accounted for more than twenty. Each killed with a slashed throat as his eyes drank in the sight of squirting arterial blood. He had never been so relaxed. He was confident that word would soon reach Fort Brazos that they were directly in his path of destruction, and when it did, that Roman would call Adrian home. He was sure the news would get there, but he wasn't depending on it; he had a plan to make absolutely certain. It would be implemented soon. It might be overkill, but Rex wasn't taking any chances. Getting Adrian to come home was the keystone in his master plan; everything else depended on it.

CHAPTER 7

MARCH 9, MORNING

L INDA AROSE EARLY AND HEADED for Roman's house. Adrian had asked her to come by, as he had something he wanted to discuss with her. She was instantly curious, but held her questions. Linda arrived and was soon having hot tea with Adrian and Sarah and Roman while Scott played with Bear in the living room.

Adrian blew on the tea, took a sip, and set the cup down. "From the looks of things, this is going to be a hard fight, and one we can't afford to lose. We lose this, and we're all dead—or those that survive will wish they were dead. It's going to take the total efforts of every able-bodied person we have, and that still leaves us badly outnumbered. I'm not just talking about the men; the women are going to have to fight, too. So will every child that is old enough to aim and pull a trigger, if a last ditch defense occurs. I want your advice on what I'm thinking.

"My plan, such as it is right now, is to take all of the able-bodied men into the field and attack the raiders as far away from here as possible. What that does, though, is leave the infirm, the children, and the women here in the village. If our men don't stop them, those who stay here will be captured or killed. So what I'm thinking is we arm everyone old enough and healthy enough that's left here and train them for a last ditch defensive battle."

Linda interrupted him, "Let me get this straight: you plan to leave the women and children and elderly here to fight against the men that will have defeated you?"

Adrian looked at her for a moment, noting that her face was turning pink and there was fire coming from her eyes. He said, "No, that's not the total plan. The plan is that the women and children and old folks will evacuate to someplace miles away. Part of that plan is to create a fighting force of the able-bodied women and older children to fight a rear guard action, if necessary, to protect the evacuation point. To protect them in their new and hidden location. It's either that, or they keep running, and that won't work; by definition, they won't be a group that can travel and survive because of the number of very young, very old, and the infirm. Whether you'll be able to come back here someday or have to start over somewhere else is anybody's guess. It's the best safety valve I can think of. The reason I asked for your advice is that I'm hoping that you three can come up with a better plan."

The four sat in silence for several minutes. Then Linda said, "That plan stinks, but I'll be damned if I can think of a better one...for now. Roman, Sarah, got any better ideas?"

Sarah said, "Unfortunately, no."

Roman shook his head silently with a grim expression.

Adrian waited a minute and then said, "All right,

then, until a better plan comes along, we'll need to get started on this one." Patton said, "'A good plan implemented today is better than a perfect plan implemented tomorrow.' I fully believe that. My idea is that Sarah will lead the villagers to the remote location. I think it best if none of the men that are going out to fight know where that location is. Then, if they're captured and tortured, they can't give it up. Linda, I believe you're the best choice to lead the rear guard fighters. I don't know you all that well, but what I have seen leads me to believe you're mentally and physically tough enough for it. You two willing to take these jobs on?"

Sarah said, "I'll get started today, talking to the people I know won't be going out. There is a pecan orchard—"

"Hush!" Adrian said quickly, interrupting her. "I don't want to know where it is, either. I don't believe any man can stand up to torture if the person doing the torture is skilled. I've seen a few instances of that."

Sarah replied, "Sorry, I wasn't thinking. Anyway, I know of a good enough place—it's quite a ways away from here and not likely to be found."

Linda impatiently said, "I can shoot and usually hit what I aim at, but I don't know anything about fighting tactics. I'm a farmer. I've never been in a gunfight of any kind. Never shot at a man before. I don't know anything about leading a combat team. Surely one of your Army buddies would be much better?"

Adrian looked into her eyes. "Any rational person would have your doubts. If I left one of the men to lead you ladies into combat, I am afraid he would be too conservative, too unwilling to risk women's lives.

It's a cultural failure we have in this country, men are over-protective of women. It goes against a man's grain to put women into harm's way. A woman, on the other hand, won't have those un-natural ideas about leading women. A woman leader will be more objective, even clinical, in doing what has to be done using other women.

"I also believe that women will trust a woman leader more readily than they will a man. Besides that, just about everyone else has attachments to the people that will be left in the village, and that will hamper their thinking. You have only your son here, and I think that enhances your ability to think clearly. You won't be hampered in the way others would. The main thing a leader has to be able to do is coldly assess and evaluate their troop's ability and the enemy's capabilities. To see the big picture clearly and respond quickly to changes as they occur. I'm aware you have no experience at this, but I believe you have the qualities that are needed."

Adrian continued, "Don't worry about the battle tactics, I'll drill you until your eyes bleed, and then when the bullets fly, you'll react correctly. It's not brain surgery; it's a matter of keeping your head when the fighting starts. I think you'll do that just fine."

Linda took a sip of tea, her hand trembling a bit. "That's an awful lot of believing that you're doing on my behalf. I'm not at all sure you're right, and if you're not, what happens to those of us you leave behind? You're pushing a huge amount of responsibility on me, and I have no background to determine if you're right or wrong. If I accept, I have to blindly believe everything you've told me, and I'm not good at blindly believing anything."

Adrian said, "You see? That's exactly what I'm talking about. You're looking at this clearly and objectively and not being persuaded merely because I'm trying to persuade you. Are you aware of how rare that is? Can you pick out a better woman leader from the available women?"

Linda looked down at her tea and thought for a long moment. "No, I can't, but I've only been here a short time and don't know the women that well."

Sarah reached over and squeezed Linda's hand briefly. "I know every one of them, and none of them would be as good for this as you. I would follow you without hesitation; I can't say that about any other woman in the village."

Adrian said, "Let's do this. You take command, and if after a few days in the position you want to appoint someone else that you think will do a better job, I'll back you up. You'll get a chance to see the women in training, evaluate them from a new perspective. If you identify a better candidate, then we'll make the change. But you have to make that decision within a week, or it'll be too late to make the change effectively. Deal?"

Linda looked hard at Adrian. He was aware of her inner turmoil, so he waited patiently for her to sort her thoughts out. She finally said, "I have to tell you that I resent being put in this spot. I just arrived here recently and now you want to put all of this responsibility on me. I don't like it one bit. But I also realize that it isn't you that created this situation—it just is what it is—so if you think I am the person you need for this, then I'll go along with it for a few days and see what happens. I am agreeing with full reservations, though."

Adrian replied, "Understood and appreciated. I know that I have thrown you a hell of a lot in just a few minutes. Most people who have this level of responsibility in a war have had years to prepare for it. Most people would have been in a military career with years of training, would be there because that's what they wanted for themselves. And here, I'm throwing this at you without warning, expectation, or any desire on your part for it. It's a lot to consider. I get that, and I'm sorry to ask this of you. But I need the absolute best we have available, and in my eyes—backed up by Sarah, by the way—you are the absolute best available here. Frankly, I think you would be the absolute best in any group anywhere under similar conditions, based on how you handled the raider situation when it came upon you, and how you took your son across country and survived. I don't see this as picking the best of a bad lot; I see this as being damn lucky someone of your caliber happens to be available. I know it's a lot to ask, but the life of everyone that will be left behind in the village has to depend on someone, and you are heads and shoulders above anyone else here. I know many of the villagers, and have Sarah, Roman and Matt's opinions on the ones I don't know. I understand your reservations and accept them. I am convinced, though, that once I start training you, you'll understand that it really is up to you, not someone else. You'll be able to evaluate these folks in action and see for yourself. Sometimes, you just get hard stuff thrust on you because you're the best available, and this is one of those times. I'm sorry, but that's the way it is."

Linda studied Adrian's eyes for a long moment, judging whether or not he was being sincere. Ultimately, her instincts told her that he was playing it straight. She responded, "That's quite a speech, and it's also quite complimentary. But speeches and compliments do not change facts, and I have to look at this from a factual basis, not an emotional one. I stand by what I said: I'll take it on with full reservations that if I find a better person for the job, then that person takes over. If after one week I cannot honestly say someone else can do it better, then I'll continue on...if you still think I'm the best person for it after you've seen me in operation for a week. That's the best I can give you right now."

Before Adrian could reply, Sarah spoke. "Linda, I've raised Adrian since he was eight years old. You've only known me for a couple of weeks and Adrian for a couple of days. If it is of any help to you, I can promise you that he is sincere and honest. I can't remember ever catching him in a lie, even as a little boy. Whenever he did wrong, he didn't avoid responsibility or try to talk his way out of it. He took whatever consequences he had coming and never once tried to lie his way out. I'm well aware of how rare that is, and how you have little reason to believe it. I'm just telling you what I know for what little peace of mind you can get out of this. It's a hard thing he's asking you. But I'm asking you, too, and for the same reason. I know the women in this village, and I know a little about you. What I know of you makes me trust you, and I'm willing to trust you with my life, and my grandchildren's lives. I can't imagine any stronger way to put it than that. You're the best we have for this."

Linda reached across the table and squeezed Sarah's hand. "Thank you, Sarah. Thank you very much. That means more than you know. I realize, too, that you and the entire village are placing a lot of trust in me, and that's an honor as high as any I have ever imagined. I'll do the best I can for a week, and then we'll see from there. Okay?"

Sarah and Adrian simultaneously said, "Okay."

MARCH 9, LATE AFTERNOON

Roman addressed the villagers, who had all gathered in the village square at his request.

Roman stood in front of the crowd. "The reason I asked you here is to give you a vote on whether or not you want Adrian or someone else to lead us in this war against the raiders. I called him home to lead us, but I won't be the only one following him—or following someone else we choose. Obviously, my vote is for Adrian. I'm his uncle, I raised him since he was eight years old, so I'm clearly biased.

"This is a life or death situation. When we fight, if we choose to fight, some of us will die. I think that's a given fact. So you have an absolute right to choose who you will follow. Your very life depends on who you follow. Therefore, let me hear any nominations for a leader. Nominate yourself or someone else. If anyone has an alternative plan, please raise your hand." There was a long silence, and no hands were raised. "Please do not be shy about this, it's too important. Anyone with any nomination, please raise your hand."

After another long silence, one hand was tentatively raised way in the back. "Yes?" Roman said. "Who's your nominee?" A voice from the back said, "Adrian, of course."

Roman said, "All right, then, let's have a show of hands for those who are willing to follow Adrian."

All hands went up; it was a unanimous vote. Roman said, "Then I'll step back and let Adrian take it from here." Roman moved back. Adrian stepped forward and began speaking.

"As you all know, there are one hundred and eighty heavily armed and savage barbarians heading for us. They are two to three weeks out. We have few options, and none of them are great. I'll lay them out for you. Option one: we sit here hoping they go away. Option two: we fight them here if they don't go away. Option three: we take all able-bodied men and attack them as far from here as we can, attempting to destroy them before they get here. And option four: we evacuate the village and let them have it, then re-establish somewhere else, hoping they don't come after us again once they decide they aren't cut out to be farmers.

"If we decide to attack them in the field, we have two choices for those who stay behind. One, they stay here and hope we win. Two, they evacuate to a place far away in case we don't win. These decisions have to be made today, here, right now. There's no time for delay. What I would like is for you all to take an hour to discuss it with your wives and husbands and friends. At the end of that hour, I'll answer questions for half an hour or so. Then we'll have a show of hands. But remember, there is one other personal option you have: you as individuals or families can choose to leave on your own. You also need to understand that if you do choose that route, I doubt you would ever be welcomed back here again by the ones who stayed and fought. So if you leave—which you are certainly free to do—it should be with the understanding that you won't be allowed to come back here to live. If you won't stand and fight for survival with us now, then you won't be allowed to take protection later from those that did."

With that, Adrian walked over to sit with Roman, Sarah, and Linda.

The buzz of talk started slowly, but built into a loud murmur. Roman and Sarah were quiet, their decision already made. Linda looked at Adrian with piercing eyes, her jaw jutting out slightly and said, "I have just one question. Are you planning on coming back alive if you don't win?"

Adrian smiled at her, enjoying her directness. "Not a chance. If we lose, it won't be because I gave up for any reason short of being killed. We simply cannot afford to lose. Nothing short of winning is acceptable. If we lose we'll all die at their hands anyway, it'll be better to go down fighting than to go down begging."

Linda replied, "I just want to know—my son's life is largely dependent on you and these men. I could leave right now, taking my son with me. We traveled before and it was rough, but not as rough as staying here to fight is going to be. We could make do, find another place to live."

Adrian asked her, "Why aren't you going, then?"

Linda replied, "Believe me, it's tempting. But wherever we go, we'll likely face raiders again at some point. Eventually we'll be in this spot again, but I doubt we'll be in a place with this many people that can fight back or with leaders that know how to fight back effectively. Our odds of winning are better here than anywhere else I've been, and if we win this battle against this many raiders, I doubt we'll ever be attacked by anyone again. Our people will be battle experienced and organized and the news of this victory will spread everywhere. After this battle, if we win, this will be the safest place there is. It's also a good place to raise Scott."

Adrian nodded. "Good logic." Then he sat quietly, waiting.

Adrian had more doubts than Linda did. He didn't know the true capability of these men. They were tough; they had to be to survive. They were definitely survivors, but survival and war are elementary opposites. In war, a man is called upon to do the exact opposite of what a good survivor does. Survival mostly consists of avoiding trouble whenever possible. War requires a man to go directly and deliberately into harm's way. These men who demonstrated strong survival instincts just by their still being alive—would they overcome that instinct and fight instead? He wouldn't know—couldn't know—until it was far too late to change strategy.

He didn't know the capability of the raiders in a pitched battle, either. They had at least demonstrated a desire to kill, to face other people and deliberately kill them. Whether they had ever faced a truly tough enemy force or not, he didn't know. Maybe they would fold at their first encounter with a determined and armed enemy, or maybe not. They had the advantage of numbers. Adrian's men were outnumbered two to one, and by men who were vicious beyond description and would show absolutely no mercy. *Well, neither will I.* He was confident on at least that point.

One of the possibilities was that the raiders could engage the villagers in battle and then split their own forces. They could send a hundred men against the village while keeping the village men in the field fighting. He couldn't see the shape or the outcome of the battle, whether it would go for or against them. The stakes were as high as they could possibly get; losing would mean the death or slavery of every villager. Survival was tough enough without the raiders, but it would become extremely rough and uncertain under their cruel captivity.

Adrian also had recurring doubts about his own ability to lead. He had successfully led small groups of extremely skilled and dedicated soldiers on strictly defined missions. He had led the Colorado villagers successfully against the cannibals. He had also led the original Fort Brazos inhabitants against that crazy ex-wrestler Mad Jack, but back then he had been cocky, had had no doubt of his own invincibility. What they had pulled off then had been based largely on luck and an unbelievable amount of confidence. Confidence that in hindsight he realized they didn't own, but had borrowed. This was different, though. Before this, the largest stakes he'd had in a battle were his and his men's lives. In the previous Fort Brazos battle, he had been blind to the possible consequences of failure. In Colorado, it was the lives of people he didn't know. Here, the stakes were his family, his friends, and his village. Here, the stakes were everyone and everything. This was literally a do or die situation; there would be no outside help, no cavalry coming to the rescue, no one to back these men up as they fought for their existence.

Adrian didn't know if he and his men were truly capable of pulling this off. He mulled over these doubts, knowing that the last thing he could do—or would do—would be to show his doubts. The only thing he was positive about was that if anything defeated these men and women, it would not be their leader showing doubt—they deserved better than that. If he showed doubt, it would inject fear into them that they didn't need to deal with. That kind of fear would be debilitating, if not annihilating. They looked to him for confidence, placed their trust in his confidence. He knew that this was the biggest acting job he had ever taken on, so he would do it well. If nothing else, he would do that one thing well. That included not sitting here looking morose, he reminded himself. So Adrian sat and waited patiently, allowing no shadow of a doubt to flicker across his face as his people kept turning to look at him while they talked it out amongst themselves.

Shortly before the hour was up, the talking slowed to a near stop. Adrian took that as his cue to resume, then stood up and walked back to his spot. "Most of you don't know me, so personal questions are fair to ask. Who wants to go first?"

From the back of the crowd came a woman's voice. "Is it true you sired bear cubs up there in the mountains?" Adrian's face immediately turned bright red from embarrassment, and the tension of the last hour was broken with an uproar of laughter from the crowd. Adrian raised both hands in defeat and the laughter slowly died down. Adrian said, "I didn't mean *that* personal." It was the right reply, and the crowd roared with laughter again. Adrian, knowing they needed this break in tension, took it on the chin and waited, smiling.

A tall man with ramrod posture stood up in the back and said, "I have a question, but it's not for you, it's for everyone else. We need to get started on this, and I just want to see a show of hands of who's willing to go out and fight." He stuck his own hand up high and was quickly followed by every man, woman, and child in the village doing the same. Then he turned to Adrian and said, "Ok, now that that's settled, General Bear, what do you want us to do and when do you want us to do it?" The crowd murmured in approval.

Adrian let them go on for a moment and then raised his hands for silence. The crowd quickly settled down, and for a brief moment, it was dead quiet. "Here's the plan..."

MARCH 10, EARLY AFTERNOON

Adrian counted the men. Ninety-seven able-bodied men with whatever arms they owned were in the town square. Nearly half were from outlying farms outside the village, but dependent on it in one way or another. Adrian addressed them, "Here's the drill: we're going to break up into five groups, each with a captain and a lieutenant. I've already selected the captains. They will immediately begin to train their groups. These ten captains are all solid leaders, some with previous military training. They will choose their own lieutenants from among their men. Every man's name has been placed into a hat. The captains will take turns drawing names at random and calling them out. As your name is called, fall in behind the captain who called it. At the end of the process, I may switch some men around to even things out in terms physical fitness or fighting skills. I want each group to be as evenly balanced as possible. When that's settled, you'll go off and train in separate areas. At the end of the second day of training, your captain will choose one of you to be his lieutenant. Any questions? Okay, captains line up, pass the hat back and forth, and start calling out names."

Adrian then walked over to the women's group. Addressing them, he said, "I count forty-four able-bodied women. You'll be under the command of Colonel Fremont. She will organize you however she sees fit. Once you're organized, I'll be in temporary command as your drill instructor. When the training regimen is underway, Colonel Fremont will take over full command again and continue the training. She will choose the captains and lieutenants in whatever manner she considers best. Colonel Fremont, you are in command. I'll return in an hour to begin the training."

Linda spoke. "General Bear, may I have a word with you?" She lowered her voice so that only Adrian could hear her. "Really, Adrian? Colonel? You only made captains of the men, and—" Adrian interrupted her. "Yes, Colonel. You will be acting autonomously; you will not have the benefit of counsel or a higher leader to turn to during battle. Your rank is higher than the men's because they will have those two advantages and you will not. You're going to make hard fast decisions without anyone to help you make them. You will be entirely on your own. These women need to know that you have a higher rank because you command a higher rank, given the situation that you and they will be in. Believe me, when the fighting starts, they will trust you with their lives, and they want to believe—have to believe—that you can be trusted; that you won't do something stupid that will get them killed without reason. They'll be watching you like a hawk in this training phase, and if you don't act the part, they'll get scared and won't fight half as well. If you have to, fake complete confidence for their benefit." Adrian didn't add that he was doing the same.

Adrian took two steps back and snapped a salute to Linda, turned on his heel, and marched back over to the men. She watched him walk away with mixed feelings of doubt and confidence. She knew his advice was right; she would have to hide her doubts from her troops.

CHAPTER 8

MARCH 10, LATE AFTERNOON

ADRIAN HAD SPENT SEVERAL HOURS with Linda's troops setting up a basic training regimen. He gave her a sheet of paper with the training plan he wanted her to carry out with the understanding that she could change it as she saw fit. Linda also watched the men training and realized quickly that there was little difference between the two regimens. The men spent more time on attack tactics than the women, who spent more time on defensive tactics. Given their respective assignments, it made sense.

Linda had chosen her second in command, Shirley—Sarah's daughter—based on observation. Shirley was aggressive and confident, taking to the drills as though it were second nature to her.

Linda explained to Shirley, "The most important skill we can learn right now is firearms competence. Each person has to be able to use their weapon with enough skill that they can hit a man at a hundred yards. So we'll spend enough time practicing to make that happen. First, we run them through the basics of shooting without ammunition. Dry firing because we need to conserve ammunition. After they have the basics down solidly, they'll be issued twenty live rounds to sight in and to practice with. If they can't make it with those twenty rounds, they'll be washed out. Better to not have incompetent shooters when the time comes than to waste ammunition."

After several hours of basic rifle and shooting instructions, Linda had a fair idea of who would be successful, and only four or five women that she didn't expect to make the cut. Those women would become field medics, given different training from Jennifer's medical group.

On the firing line, Linda shouted, "Remember BRASS: *Breathe* in and let half your breath back out and hold half in your lungs; *Relax* your major muscle groups, as tense muscles will cause you to miss; *Aim* by picking a small portion of the target you want to hit, aim for a button if you can see one, or choose the center of the largest part of the target, and do not aim at the whole target; your *Sight* picture should be the alignment of three things, the rear sight will be aligned correctly with the front sight, and the target point you have chosen will be directly above and sitting on top of the front sight; and *Squeeze* the trigger slowly while maintaining your sight picture until the rifle fires. If you do it correctly, you'll be somewhat surprised when the rifle does fire. If you jerk the trigger, you will pull the rifle off of the target and waste the shot.

"Then put another round in the chamber unless you're using a semi-automatic rifle, acquire another target, and repeat the process. It is critical that you do not rush or get panicked. Slow, consistent, accurate fire is far more effective than slinging bullets and hoping for the best. You'll be under intense pressure—worse than anything you've ever experienced in your life—when they're coming at you shooting. Your adrenaline will be pumping, your mind will be panicky, and your fine motor skills will be out the window. In the heat of battle, you may develop tunnel vision. Presence of mind is what will kill the bastards; the bullet you send will be the agent of your presence of mind. How accurate and deadly you are is a direct result of remaining calm and following a sound shooting procedure. Remaining calm and following procedure is the most powerful weapon you have. Any questions before we commence the dry firing exercise?"

One hand went up. "Yes? Your question?"

One of the women stood and said, "I've heard that dry firing can damage a gun, is that not true?"

Linda replied, "That's a good question. Sometimes, yes, it will, but most times it won't—it depends largely on the type of gun you have. To be on the safe side, we have taken an empty casing for each of your rifles and replaced the primer with a piece of melted plastic for the firing pin to hit. Those will be issued to you momentarily. Any other questions?" After a moment of silence, she said, "No? Captain, pass out the practice rounds."

MARCH 10, EVENING

Adrian, Linda, Jennifer, Sarah, and Roman were seated around Sarah's dinner table. The dishes had been cleared and stacked in the sink. Adrian and Roman were sipping Roman's reserve whisky without ice. The women had all chosen hot tea.

Adrian said, "Roman, this is the best ever. You're a distilling genius."

Roman replied, "Practice, practice, practice. That's all it takes. Next year, I'm going to make wine from the wild mustang grapes, then distill that down into cognac. I think it'll be good. How did the training go today?"

Adrian replied, "For the men, at least, it went well. We began covering advance and cover techniques. We only spent a little time on actual shooting technique because these men already know how to shoot. Hell, they're all hunters, or they wouldn't have survived this long. What we covered was taking the time to draw a bead and squeezing it off while under fire, not getting excited to the point that they get buck fever and just start banging away. Hunting is one thing; shooting while being shot at is something intensely different. We spent most of our shooting time on that concept. Tomorrow, we're going to work on advance and cover some more, then start on simple ambush techniques. The men are extremely motivated, so the lessons are going faster than I had hoped they might." Adrian looked at Linda and asked, "How about your troop, Linda?"

"It went quite well. As I had guessed, there were four who couldn't hit the target to save their lives, literally speaking. What I intend to do is make them medics. It's not that they aren't brave, and with enough time and ammunition I'm sure they could learn to shoot well enough, but there isn't enough time or ammunition for that. Jennifer, tomorrow those four will be at the hospital for basic trauma training. Would you see to it that they are versed in that and provide them with field kits to work with?"

Jennifer replied, "Certainly. I'll need at least a week with them. But I thought the nurses and I would be performing that duty? Not that anyone said so, but I did assume it."

Adrian spoke up. "Actually, what we will need you to do is act as a field M.A.S.H.-type unit. The field medics will do what they can in the field, and then the wounded will be carried to you for more advanced treatment. From there, they will be carried back here to the hospital for continued care. It's a three-step system that will provide the best possible chance of recovery. My thinking is that you'll set up a temporary field hospital between the battle site and the village. You'll need to be at that field hospital to receive and treat the incoming wounded. Once they are stabilized, they'll be carried to the village hospital for continued care in a better setting. What do you think?"

"Sounds reasonable, but who is going to do all that carrying? You're going to be pulling able-bodied men away from the fighting to do that, aren't you?"

"Yes, but just as Linda has recognized a better use for some of her soldiers, so have I. Just because they are male doesn't mean they are automatically fierce fighters. Before the grid dropped, the majority of America's men would not have made good fighters. After the grid dropped, those men mostly died off. The men who did survive, for the most part, were the ones who had the fighter instinct. Not all of them, though, and a few of the men would be more dangerous to us than to the enemy in a fight. I don't have a lower opinion of those men than the others—they are just different, and it's probably the result of factors they had no control over. As Linda said, it's not that they aren't brave or that they don't want to fight. Medics are, in my estimation, the bravest of all. Their mission is as critical and necessary as any other, but they are even more exposed to a hostile line-of-fire environment and risk their own lives solely to help their comrades. So, in short, I'll assign some of my men to act as medics and stretcher-bearers. I'll have these men at your hospital in a couple of days after I've identified them all."

MARCH 11, MORNING

Matthew had taken a wood-gas-fired truck into Waco. He'd had an idea for the training and explained it to Adrian. Upon his return, he told Adrian, "We had good luck. No one has seen any use for these since the grid dropped, so there were plenty of them, and plenty of ammo, too. I'm afraid the paintballs may have hardened up over the years, but they will shoot, and perhaps sting all the more for it."

Adrian replied, "When you first suggested it I thought it was pretty silly, but the idea grew and I realized it was a good one. Will we have any problems firing these things?"

"No. They work on compressed gas, and the gas cylinders hold their pressure nearly forever. I tried a few and they worked fine. Using the old phone book, I located three large supply sources and brought back a truckload. More than enough for several exercises. This was still a popular sport when the grid went down. I can go back for more if need be. I also looked for real guns and ammo, but didn't find squat—those were picked off long ago."

"All right, then, let's get this show on the road—"

Matt interrupted. "I also picked up components for the pipe cannons. One of the ideas I'm going to try out is loading them with short pieces of chainsaw blade chain; they have wicked sharp teeth. I found loads of chainsaw chains at two of the home improvement chain stores—no pun intended," Matt said with a big grin. "I can cut these short so they can then be curled up into tight little sections that will load easily into the cannon. When they're shot out, they should straighten out and then fly through the air end over end, chopping through the raiders like crazy. My idea is to test this a couple of times, getting an idea of the spread pattern. Then the cannons will be spaced out to get a continuous field of shrapnel across the segment the raiders will approach and a specific distance where the maximum damage will occur. They'll be fired with electronic igniters similar to the one I used in the hog gun I showed you. So picture this: the cannons are pre-set at the right distance apart. The distance where the chains spread out from each cannon to provide a continuous field of damage is marked on the ground with, say, green-painted rocks. The raiders come charging in, and when they get to those rocks, the women simultaneously fire the cannons.

"The chains come flying out, unfold, and zoom through the air at waist height, providing a solid line of flying steel across the width of the raiders. The result will be devastating. A lot will depend on the raiders being bunched together and we can't completely control that, but the carnage will be horrendous. One downside the black powder will create a dense cloud of smoke. There will be a few moments where the women won't be able to see the raiders, but the raiders won't be able to see the women, either. How long that lasts depends on wind speed at the time. On a calm day, it could be two or three minutes. What do you think?"

Adrian replied, "I think I am very damned happy you're on our side. I think it's brilliant. Let me know how you're progressing and if you need any help."

"The only help I'll need will be some extra hands turning out black powder for two days. The rest I can do myself fairly easily."

Adrian said, "I'll get some of the men and women who will be acting as stretcher bearers to your shop first thing in the morning."

Later that morning, Adrian assembled all the troops, men and women alike. He announced, "As part of the training, Matthew had a brilliant idea. He went into town and came back with enough paintball guns, gas cylinders, and ammo to run several drills. At first, you may think it sounds a bit ridiculous, but after a moment, the brilliance of it shines through. It beats the hell out of running around shouting *bang, bang*! We're going to divide into two groups: aggressors and defenders. The women will defend Fort Brazos against the men. This will give excellent practice with the added benefit of knowing who was wounded or killed. We'll get practice in as near a live fire environment as we can without actually killing each other.

"On top of that, we'll be able to practice battle field communications, medical treatment and evacuation, and how best to defend the fort. We won't be trying to capture a flag as in the usual war games. We will be continuing the exercise until one side has no survivors.

It's to be a war to the death for each side. These old paint balls might or might not burst when they hit. They will sting either way. The only safety device will be eye shields, we don't need to lose any eyeballs in this practice. If you are hit, even if the paint doesn't explode on you, you are to lie down and wait for the medics to find you and carry out their mission. Medics are fair game to shoot, just like they will be shot at when we actually fight. Any questions? None? Okay, captains take your men east of the fort and prepare your invasion. Colonel Fremont, as soon as the men are out of sight, take your defensive positions. Men, in this first exercise, you will imitate the known tactics of our enemy as explained to you in the briefings. This will not only give the defenders a realistic view of how they would be attacked, but will also give you firsthand knowledge of the strengths and weaknesses of the tactics you'll be fighting against. Subsequent exercises will use our tactics and strategies, the ones we'll be using against them. Defenders, you'll also be involved in all exercises to keep you from getting into one set way of thinking, because the attackers will have any number of ways of coming at you."

MARCH 11, AFTERNOON

Linda's advance sentries began filtering in from their observation posts, relaying the incoming attackers' positions and movements. Using this intel, Linda made subtle but important adjustments to the defensive positions.

Linda watched through binoculars as the men moved in. "Shirley, notify the squad leaders they have ten minutes before they see the attackers. Remind them of the effective range of their paintball guns, to rely on the landmarks we identified for ranging information, and that they are not to fire until the attackers reach the optimum range and target density. Stay with them and move from position to position giving advice and confidence."

Adrian stood by silently, also watching with binoculars. They had taken a position on a rooftop where they could watch without being seen. Linda would be actively moving her troops as needed and issuing commands by runner. Adrian would only observe, offering no advice or counsel. He would instead watch everything and make his observations known in the post-exercise briefing.

The attackers followed the known tactics of the raiders. First, they sent out scouts to observe. The information was relayed to the fighters and they gathered into three distinct groups. They came at the Fort on a dead run, firing as they came. It was a classic three-front strategy, hitting the fort from three directions, putting the defenders in a crossfire while minimizing the chances of friendly fire hitting their own.

The attack was fast, furious, and brutal, and the battle lasted less than five minutes. Many of the attackers were cut down in the initial surge with few losses to the defenders. However, the attackers still overran the defenders and quickly eliminated them. The attackers won, although with heavy losses.

At the follow-up briefing, Adrian said, "We learned a lot today. Thank you, Matthew—it was an excellent idea that will save us many lives before this is over. We learned that the defensive positions need to be fortified more than they are. We learned that the defenders have a chance to succeed if we do several things differently, and those ideas will be incorporated into the next exercise. We also learned that the attack force must be cut down in size considerably if the defenders are to have a chance of success—that will be on the men's shoulders. Our goal is to eliminate them entirely, and I plan on achieving that goal, but as a fall back, we have to be realistic about how many raiders have to be killed in order to give the defenders at the village a solid chance to win.

"Each of you as an individual has learned a lot. It isn't a realistic live fire exercise in the important ways, of course, but it is as close as we're going to get to the real thing. Some of you, due to age or physical condition, can't keep up with the main group. That's no slight, it's just a fact, and we have to face facts. I've identified most of those individuals. In subsequent exercises, I'll confirm those and probably add some more. Those men will be segregated out into a separate group to act as stretcher-bearers to assist the medics and take a load off their shoulders, allowing them more time to work on the wounded.

"Roman—you, Perry, Matt, and Tim's mission will be to supplement the frontline fighting troops with actions that delay, harass, and kill the enemy in smaller micro-actions. Your primary mission will be to slow the attackers, buying the main group more time to get set up. You will be the first force to encounter the enemy in combat. Your final mission will be to engage any enemy flanks that you can reach during the battle. Be aware your mission is not only critical, but requires the utmost of bravery; you'll be four men acting independently against almost two hundred enemy combatants. You'll be outnumbered fifty to one. Do not for a moment think you are being relegated to a lesser mission."

CHAPTER 9

JANUARY 27, DAWN

REX SELECTED TWO MEN AND had them brought to his tent. "Each of you has a mission coming up, a mission that requires strict obedience while acting entirely on your own. 'Acting' is a good word for this mission, because you will be actors. Pay close attention and I'll go over it as many times as it takes for you to be comfortable with your role, and I'll answer any questions you have. You have to get this exactly right. You will be dressed as farmers and will go into Fort Brazos pretending that you are fleeing ahead of us. You will pretend to be a refugee and will tell them that we appear to be heading straight for them. You'll stay only a couple of hours, asking for food and water. Then you'll leave, heading west as though continuing your flight. Your missions are secret. You will not say anything to anyone about what you are doing. You know what will happen if you do."

"You", he said pointing at the first man, startling him, "You will leave in the morning and get there as fast as you can. You'll tell them you had a small farm just outside of Woodville, Texas that was burned to the ground. If you happen to run across anyone from that area that questions you, you can say something like, 'Look, I came here to warn you, and I didn't have to. I'm out of here, you ungrateful son of a bitch.' Then leave—remember, heading west. When you are well away from the village, circle around and come back here."

"And you," Rex said, pointing to the second man, "You will do the same thing, except you'll leave in three days and you're from a small farm near Diboll, Texas. You will add one other piece of information to your story. You will say that while hiding, you overheard two of the raiders mention Fort Brazos. You didn't hear anything else clearly, you don't know their mission or why they even mentioned Fort Brazos, you just heard one of them say it to another one.

"Here's the fascinating thing for both of you: you've been selected for a number of reasons, not the least of which is that you have family in Baton Rouge. Fail in your mission, and I send word back to kill your families, and not in a nice way, either. Succeed, and after we take Fort Brazos, you can go home to your family right away if you want to. Now, is that clear enough?"

FEBRUARY 8, MORNING

Rex strode into his tent, impatiently telling the radio operator, "This had better be damn good, or you'll regret sending for me!"

The operator, shaken, started to speak, then cleared his throat and tried again. "I just heard Roman talking to Adrian on the radio. Roman asked Adrian to come home as fast as possible, that he was needed badly because there's trouble heading toward Fort Brazos. Adrian said he could be there in about three weeks. Roman didn't specify what the trouble was, just told him to hurry and not talk to anyone on the way."

Rex, smiling his big, nerve-wracking smile, asked, "Adrian said he would come? Are you completely sure?"

"Yes sir, he said he would leave today, as soon as he gathered up some gear. There's no doubt about it, he's heading home today."

Rex said, "And you haven't told anyone? This is still our little secret?"

"No sir, not a soul. I haven't said anything to anyone, just as you ordered."

Rex's smile grew even larger and scarier. "Good work. Step outside a minute—I want to praise you in front of the men."

When they were outside the tent, Rex called some of the men over. "Men, I want you to witness this." Rex pulled his knife out and slit the radio operator's throat so fast that his hand was a blur of motion. He watched as the operator's blood jetted while his heels drummed the ground, until they slowly stopped. "This is what happens to men who fail in their mission. Remember it. Get this body out of here, and then throw his radio junk out of my tent."

Rex went back into his tent and sat in his camp chair. He didn't need the radio or the operator any longer; Adrian was heading for Fort Brazos, and it had been confirmed. He thought briefly of the radio operator. Just that much less junk to haul around, and another opportunity to instill fear in his men while also letting off a little steam. *A good day,* he thought to himself, *a very good day indeed.*

After the radio equipment had been removed and Rex was alone, he once again pulled out his "Adrian bag" and began fondling its contents. That night as he lay in bed waiting for sleep, he went through his plan for Adrian step by step. He looked for any weakness, any hole, but found none. He slept a deep, contented sleep.

CHAPTER 10

MARCH 12, AFTERNOON

THE TRAINING EXERCISE THAT DAY followed a different plan. The number of attackers had been reduced by half to get an idea of the maximum number the defenders could handle. The defenders had also utilized every lesson they had learned from the first exercise, while the attackers utilized the enemies' tactics again. It was still a close battle, but this time the defenders won, although with still heavy losses.

After the conclusion of the exercise, Adrian said to Linda, "Your troops are learning and adapting quickly, I'm very impressed with them. I feel vindicated in asking you to lead them." While Adrian was talking to her, he was growing uncomfortably aware of feelings he had never expected again, and those feelings, in turn, caused him to feel guilt. He felt like he was betraying Alice, but didn't have control over it. This conflict caused Adrian to speak more harshly than he wanted to, though he knew that these feelings weren't Linda's fault, she wasn't coming on to him in any way.

Linda immediately noticed the undue harshness of

his tone, not understanding why he was giving praise in that rough way. Adrian asked stiffly, "You've had time to consider relegating leadership to someone else. Have you arrived at a conclusion?"

Linda was worried by the enormity of the role she was playing and her extensive self-doubts of her ability to perform under fire. These should have been enough for anyone to deal with, she thought, yet on top of that, she also had to deal with her involuntary but undeniable growing attraction to Adrian. Not only was he attractive, but she sensed an undercurrent of emotional vulnerability, and that started a chain reaction of feelings that were moving rapidly out of her control. Whenever she was near him, she found herself acting almost mean, suppressing feelings she was uncomfortable with and didn't want him to know about.

Linda sighed, then responded, "Yes, I'll continue to lead them, it wouldn't be fair to them to make a change now, and I think you knew this would happen the night you talked me into it. You manipulated me and I still resent it. These women are not only brave, but they are fighting for their loved ones—their children, mostly. There isn't any stronger motivation in the world than that. Women can be as effective fighters as men are, and I've been thinking that maybe you should utilize the best of them, and me, in the direct fighting."

Adrian was surprised at this suggestion, but hid it and replied, "I know women can be excellent fighters. I've spent a lot of time overseas where women fight alongside men. I have no doubts of their capabilities, having faced some and also fought alongside some of them. But in those cultures, they've had generations to adapt to the idea. Here, it's different. Women have been placed on pedestals since the beginnings of the country, and men here have false ideas about women's fighting abilities. What I'm afraid of is that our men will be less effective if they are fighting alongside women, especially women they have relationships with.

"In the foreign armies the women are not from the men's families, or even neighbors. It's a big difference and one I can't risk, these men and women all know each other. Many intimately. It's not the ability of the women I am concerned about, but the men's effectiveness if they become over-protective of the women next to them when the bullets are flying. I do not want the men distracted in any way, and that kind of distraction could be fatal."

Linda was listening, but couldn't stop thinking his scars accentuated his attractiveness. He was virile and had undeniable presence and charisma. She tried hard to suppress her rebellious feelings as dishonorable to her husband's memory and completely inappropriate for the time and circumstances. She was also surprised by Adrian's matter of fact respect for women's abilities; she hadn't seen that coming.

Linda wasn't aware of her scowl in response to her feelings, and the scowl had no relation to Adrian's statement when she replied, "That's something I can understand. My husband would get like that sometimes, and I always hated it. I'm fully aware that I can't fight a man hand to hand and expect to win, but with a gun it's—as you say—a matter of keeping a clear head. Bullets are equal. I have to say I disagree with your decision, but I can't find fault with your reasoning."

They looked at each other for a long moment with a

tension that caused irritation between them.

Adrian finally replied, "I'm leaving in the morning to go on a scouting trip. I need to see the raiders for myself, form my own opinions and do some probing. I'm leaving you in charge of the men and women while I'm gone."

Linda's surprise at this announcement replaced the scowl. Adrian went on, "I want you to continue the training and exercises, evaluating what you see and giving me a full report when I get back. The men need to be evaluated for their ability to keep up and for any individual signs of mental or emotional weakness in a fast and furious situation. Also they need to work on battlefield communications, throw them some surprises and see how they react, pull unexpected ambushes. See if the captains can improve the speed and accuracy of communications on the fly. Your own command needs the same kind of attention— work on the runners being faster and on verbatim transmission. Commands passed by runner need to be simple, brief, uncomplicated, but they have to be precise. Surprise the women with attacks they don't know are coming, see how they react. Work on those things while I'm gone."

"You're leaving me in command of the men?" She felt a sense of intensely heightened pressure.

"Yes, Colonel. You are the highest rank, and that means you are in command while I'm gone. Don't screw it up."

"'Don't screw it up?'" she retorted with obvious anger, her face reddening. "Would you have said that to a man left in command?"

"No. To a man I would have been less polite, and

he wouldn't have asked me about it, either," Adrian responded sharply.

Linda tried to keep her face non-committal, but she was stumbling inside at being trusted with so much so fast. She said coldly, "Don't worry, General Bear, I won't fuck it up."

MARCH 13, PRE-DAWN

Adrian was packing travel rations into his backpack. He packed parched corn, cornbread, jerky, a jar of pecan butter, and a small amount of smoked ham from Sarah's pantry. It gave him an idea.

"Sarah, do you think you could create a densely nutritious battlefield ration? Something that travels well, doesn't spoil quickly, and has tons of calories? Something that doesn't require field cooking?"

She thought for a moment then replied, "Yes, I think so. I can think of a couple of approaches. One would be a food bar made of chopped pecans, cooked cornmeal and sorghum molasses. I can experiment and come up with a bar that will be a bit tough to chew but pack a calorie wallop. I doubt if it will taste very good though. Or I can use hog lard and make pemmican with dried meat and chopped dried pecans. The pemmican bars would have to be individually wrapped and sealed and won't last long."

"How long would they last?"

"In this heat and humidity, maybe a week."

"How about trying both? The pemmican would have more calories and would be eaten first, saving the molasses bars for after the pemmican is gone. If we're out there more than a week, I'll be really surprised."

"I'll work on it and get samples made up. When I get it right, I'll get the women to start making them in quantity. How many will you need?"

"Fifteen for each person going afield. As for size, about two thousand calories each, whatever size that turns out to be. We need food that doesn't require cooking or heating. Something stable, and light enough that we can carry it with us. Something we can eat on the run and keep our energy levels high. If there are any stimulants that can be added, so much the better, but the stimulants would only be in two thirds of them. The non-stimulant ones would be for night rations and marked to show the difference. Some pill type stimulants would be good for the night watches too."

"I'll talk to Jennifer about that," Sarah said. "She'll know if we have any or where we can get some, and the right dosages per bar. Two thousand calories is a lot for one meal, isn't it?"

"Yes, but these are going to be extremely high active days and we'll need a lot of energy. I'd rather they were too big than too small; we can always eat only part of it if we need to, but being short on calories would be detrimental. This will give us a slight advantage. Those raiders don't carry a lot of food, depending on raiding as they go. We're not going to give them time to raid and stockpile food once we engage them, so they'll be hungrier and weaker than us.

"Well, I'm off to meet Tim and Jerry. We'll be back in four or five days. I'll see you then."

Sarah gave him a quick hug and asked, "Tim? Isn't he a little old for a hard trip like that?"

Adrian replied, "He's in good shape for a man his age; I think he'll keep up. I want him there to look over the sniper possibilities, and maybe to pick off a few bad guys while we're out there."

"You take care of him and Jerry. Aw hell, I know you will. Be safe and come back healthy—all three of you."

———

The three men had been walking for a little over an hour, heading east to find the raiders. They were moving quickly, but not double-time, as Adrian would have preferred. He needed his two friends in good shape throughout this endeavor, and was careful not to exhaust them. There was little talking as they walked, but knowing they were far from the enemy they didn't whisper when they did talk. That would come later.

Tim was carrying his .50 caliber sniper rifle inside a strong fiberglass case that was made for it. It was a heavy and awkward load. The case was lined with a dense foam material, cut to fit the rifle and scope so that it was protected from being jarred. He also had his favorite side arm in a belt holster, a 9mm Glock. Jerry was carrying an M4 and one hundred rounds of ammunition pre-loaded into magazines that were in pouches around his waist. Since he was also carrying forty rounds of .50-caliber ammunition for Tim, he didn't carry a side arm.

Adrian also carried an M4, with one hundred rounds of ammo in magazines. His side arm was his favorite combat pistol, the unbeatable 1911 .45 caliber. His was a recent make from Springfield arms, a duplicate of the original Colt design with only a few modifications to improve it. An enlarged ejection port, a polished ramp, and an adjustable Timney trigger.

All three men carried large knives. Adrian's knife

was one he'd had custom made for him before the grid had dropped, the one he had carried and used in combat for years. It weighed a solid five pounds with a larger and thickly spined blade and heavy knob at the end of the handle. The blade was made of uniquely alloyed high carbon Damascus steel that had been phosphate coated and blued to a dull black color. The Damascus construction allowed for an extremely hard steel that was flexible instead of brittle. It was difficult to sharpen, but held a razor's edge a long time. The balance and weight had been arrived at with the knife's maker after considerable trial and error; with Adrian using several prototypes before being fully satisfied. It looked like a small machete in size if not in shape where it more or less resembled a Bowie. The knife's maker was an expert in forging samurai swords and had reluctantly taken on the project only after Adrian had worn down his defenses. Adrian had met him while training in Okinawa. The fact that the knife would actually be used in combat, and not as a showpiece put on a mantle, was the final deciding factor. The grip was classic samurai sword style, never slipping in his hands no matter how sweaty or bloody. The balance was perfect for Adrian, but awkward for most men.

They reached the eastern outskirts of Hillsboro shortly before dark. Adrian said, "We'll camp here. This will be our last night to have a fire before we begin our return. We'll find our scouts day after tomorrow at the rendezvous point. They know when to expect us, and can then point us to the raiders."

Tim, weary from the day's march, said, "You've set a pace I can maintain, I appreciate that. But if worse comes to worst, you two move on out and I'll fend for myself."

Adrian replied, "Appreciate the thought, but one thing we all have to get in our heads is that we leave no one behind, and we come back for their bodies later of those killed in action. That may sound foolish, but it's good strategy. Men fight better when they have confidence that they are never on their own. It's an advantage we'll have over the raiders. Those men know if they are wounded they're left behind, and it doesn't give them any confidence during a battle action. Our men will have that confidence; I believe it is not only right, but also smart."

Tim replied, "That's nice, Adrian, but I can damn well take care of myself. You don't spend two tours in 'Nam and then live to be my age by being a pussy. I know what I can do and what I can't do, which is more than I can say for most folks. If you get all three of us killed because you're too damn noble to have good sense, you won't be doing me or anyone else any fucking favors. So let's get this straight right here and right now before the bullets start flying: if we have to run, then the best thing is you two run one way and me another way.

"If we have time to pick a place to meet back up, fine; if not, I'll see you back at the fort. I will not be responsible for getting you two killed for some pretty little theory you have. And I sure as shit won't be letting you get me killed for it, either. Most likely, I'll have a better chance of surviving on my own if they are in hot pursuit anyway, done it before. Jesus but you modern day warriors are a bunch of ball-less wimps. You wouldn't have made a pimple on my worst man's ass back in the day."

Adrian and Jerry couldn't help laughing. When Adrian got control again, he said, "Roman told me you were a bit salty, I should have listened better. Okay, we'll do it your way if it comes to it. Let's hope it doesn't."

MARCH 14, NIGHT

Adrian took the last watch. He assigned Tim the first watch so that he would get the maximum amount of uninterrupted sleep before moving out the next morning. Jerry had the middle watch. Adrian had set their watch lengths at two hours each, giving them each six hours of sleep. Adrian took the four-hour watch. He was in better condition than the other two, and he always rose early anyway. He spent his watch hours going over his plans, tactics, and strategy, searching for weaknesses or improvements. It was productive time for him as he thought of things to change or try.

At the first sign of light, Adrian awakened the two men. They set about preparing breakfast and putting up their gear. They ate smoked ham heated in a skillet, placing the ham between two layers of warmed cornbread. It made a satisfying and filling meal, and it would be their last warm meal for several days. They washed it down with hot tea. Tim remarked, "You know, I'm starting to like this faggot tea. It's pretty good. I see why those shithead Brits love it so much now."

Adrian grinned and said, "We need to maintain our pace from yesterday. Tim, I need you fully operational when we get there. How're you feeling? Don't bullshit me, either. I would rather slow down than get there with you of limited use."

"I'm a little fucking stiff from yesterday and sleeping on the ground last night. Let me get warmed up, and then ask me again in an hour or two. I'll give you the straight dope. I'm too old to play pussy games about important shit."

Adrian smiled and said, "I believe you, oh ancient one. Jerry you, doing okay?"

Jerry replied, "Never better, cousin. Let's get this show on the road."

Two hours later, Adrian called a break. Each man took off his boots and socks. The boots were placed where the maximum amount of sunlight and wind would enter and dry them. Socks were hung on sticks to get wind and sunlight, as well.

Adrian asked Tim, "Okay, how about it, Mr. Antiquity, how're you holding up?"

Tim threw a rock at Adrian and replied, "Just fine; I can keep this piddling pace for days. I could go faster in a pinch, too."

The men examined each other's feet for blisters and hot spots, then put on fresh socks and hung the used socks on the outsides of their packs to continue airing out.

"We'll skirt around the south of Hillsboro," Adrian said. "We have no need to see the town, and we would be too exposed."

They walked until lunchtime, and then settled down for a cold meal of parched corn and jerky. They took off their boots and followed the foot hygiene drill, as they would at every break for the duration of their journey. They all knew that it would be stupid to hobble themselves with blisters, so every reasonable precaution was taken.

Later that afternoon as they continued their march, Tim spotted two men in the distance. He gave the hand signal and they all hit the ground. Adrian got out his binoculars, a powerful set made by Zeiss, and scoped out the two men.

Adrian said, "I can't tell much from this distance. Tim, how in the hell did you even see them?"

Tim replied, "It's an old man's trick. I was a prepper from way back and had Lasik surgery as part of my preparations long before the grid dropped. I thought glasses would be a bad thing to be reliant on if the shit hit the fan someday. Believe it or not, I have 20/15 in one eye and 20/10 in the other. I can see a gnat at two hundred yards and tell you if it has balls or not."

Adrian said, "I believe you. They're a long ways off and I didn't see them. I bet that vision helps with the long range shooting."

"Some, but with this scope, I probably wouldn't need better than 20/20."

"They're probably refugees fleeing from the raiders; they don't act like scouts, but we'll wait until they're closer to decide. I wouldn't want to make a mistake and assume they're not scouts if they are." Adrian said.

CHAPTER 11

MARCH 12, EVENING

REX GATHERED HIS TEAM LEADERS for a debriefing of the day's exercises. "Men, we're getting closer to Fort Brazos every day. Closer to all that food and all those women. By now, they have an idea that we are heading toward them. I expect them to send out scouts to spy on us and perhaps engage us in some tests. They'll want to see what our tactics are when attacked. If they do, it'll be a quick hit and run ambush; they won't have their full force out this far.

"I want those scouts captured alive at all costs, and I do mean at *all* costs. I want them alive—be very clear on that point. Kill one of their scouts, and you're going to have to face me. Bring them to me alive, and your reward will be extraordinary. I want them alive, all of them, for my interrogation. What they can tell me is far more important than you can imagine. If they attack, return fire as you ordinarily would, but do not aim at them, aim near them. I want them to think you are reacting normally and shooting at them. Immediately send runners up and down the line to order the nearby groups to commence encircling them.

"Those of you that will be encircling them, put out a net completely around them, dropping off men wherever appropriate, but do not fire at them unless they are trying to escape. If you fire at them, fire in front of them to try to herd them back into the circle. When the circle is complete, start drawing in closer until they surrender. I cannot stress this enough: I want them alive. I don't care how many men you lose in the process. Is that clear?"

"Yes, sir!" they all responded.

"Good," Rex replied. "Tomorrow morning we'll practice. Choose two men to act as the aggressors, live fire exercise. The two men will, of course, fire above our heads, and our return fire will be directed near to but not at them. We'll repeat this exercise until everyone reacts swiftly and correctly . I'll be observing and correcting until you get it right. Dismissed."

Rex watched the men leave as they went back to their groups. He thought, *sooner or later, Adrian will be out to scout for himself. He'll have to; it's his way to see the enemy with his own eyes before engaging. With a little luck, I might catch him early on. Maybe.*

Later that night, Rex went back to his tent and unpacked his "Adrian bag," as he thought of it, checking each item, fondling them with delight. He checked every nut and bolt on the take-apart crossbow. Rex thought back to the only time he had fought Adrian. It had been in a bar. He had watched Adrian for hours, drinking and celebrating a successful mission accomplished with his crew. Rex hadn't killed in weeks, and he was tense. Watching Adrian laughing and carrying on wound his tension up to the boiling point, and Rex had snapped.

He shouldn't have taken Adrian head on; he knew it was giving himself away, but he couldn't help it that night. Adrian had exactly one advantage over Rex: Adrian was faster. Adrian's reflex time was unbelievable, and Rex knew it. Still, he attacked, and because Adrian had been drinking a lot more than Rex, the fight was nearly even for a few moments. Rex got in several good, hard blows, blows that seemed to bounce off of Adrian with no effect. Adrian was faring no better against Rex, however.

Then Rex's foot had slipped in a wet spot, and Adrian had taken advantage of it, knocking Rex out.

Over the ensuing years, Rex had gone over and over that fight. *If I hadn't slipped*, he thought, *I would have beaten him, sure as hell.* He acknowledged that it had been a strategic error. Adrian had kept a closer eye on Rex after that. Otherwise, Rex would have surely had an opportunity to implement his plan. As it was, he tried to maintain a lower profile, waiting for Adrian's attention to fade or slip. In time, he was sure it would have, but the grid collapse had happened first, and Rex lost track of Adrian in the aftermath.

MARCH 13, EVENING

Rex watched from a hilltop as his men encircled the two mock attackers. It was the third run, and the men had finally gotten it right. The first one had been a clusterfuck, one of the men being killed in the process. The second went better, but not well enough. This one had gone smoothly, the men rapidly stringing out the net and then slowly drawing it tighter until the two aggressors had no option but to surrender or die. Rex was pleased. He wanted Adrian so bad he could taste it.

After the exercise, he would return the men to their march on Fort Brazos. Capturing Adrian wouldn't be easy, but it would be done, come hell or high water. Rex was contemplating what he would do to Adrian when his second in command cleared his throat to get Rex's attention.

"What?" Rex snapped with irritation. "What the hell do you want?"

"Orders for tomorrow, sir?" Frank replied calmly. He was used to Rex's irritability, though not quite immune to it. He knew that he maintained his high position because he was willing to confront Rex, but only to a certain degree. He was also aware there was a line that he dared not cross, and he was careful not to. He was aware that Rex valued his confrontational style because it kept things moving smoothly, and kept Rex from having to attend to the details himself. Rex's frequent mental withdrawals and emotional outbursts would otherwise have had things moving in fits and starts.

"We return to the march on Fort Brazos in the morning. These idiots took all day to get this simple exercise right. Jesus, I wish I had better men than this."

Frank replied carefully, "They're the best of a generally poor lot, sir. On the bright side, though, they are certainly killers. They don't hesitate to do that."

Rex looked at Frank for a long, tense moment. "Are you trying to tell me my business? Do you think I don't know what we have?"

Frank, not backing down the way the rest of the men would have, said, "No sir, just pointing out the facts. I'll give the order to move out in the morning as usual, sir." Not waiting to be dismissed, Frank turned to leave, thinking, *Psycho, pure psycho. But he's our psycho, and he's damned effective. I pity the poor fools at Fort Brazos.*

CHAPTER 12

MARCH 14, LATE AFTERNOON

AS THE TWO MEN DREW closer, Adrian was able to make them out. From the way they moved, taking no care to be stealthy, and their two small caliber rifles, Adrian was sure they were refugees.

Adrian whispered, "I make them out as refugees. They'll pass a little to the north of us. I don't want to waste anymore time, and talking to them would take too long. As soon as they get behind that tree line, let's move out."

They traveled the rest of the day without incident. They camped that night without a fire. After eating a cold meal, Tim pulled out a flask and took a long swig. He saw Adrian looking at him and said, "What? You've never seen a man drink before?" He took another long swig and then screwed the cap back on the flask. "Son, I was doing this shit when your dad was a puppy. I know how much to drink and when." He proffered the flask to Adrian.

Adrian took the flask, unscrewed the top, and took two short swigs, then handed it to Jerry. Jerry took it and handed it back over to Tim. "No thanks, I'll wait 'til we get back. God knows what kind of cooties you have, old man."

Tim snorted and smiled, then said, "You may have a point there, youngster, you just may have a point."

They stood the same watches as the previous night, then hit the trail early the next morning.

Two hours after sunrise, Adrian said, "There's our rendezvous point—that grove of trees just south of the water tower."

When they arrived, Adrian and his companions spread out and slowly entered the tree line. Bollinger called out from inside the grove, "Adrian, over here."

The five men joined up. Adrian asked, "How far away are they?"

Bollinger said, "A day's march will put you in sight of them."

Clif nodded in agreement.

Adrian replied, "Show me on the map. Anything new to report?"

Bollinger said, "Naw, just the same old, same old. They're moving a little faster over this flat land, but not much." After conferring over the map, Adrian said, "Ok, you two go back and send out the next two. We'll meet them at the farm with the big red barn. The one next to Highway 22, by the creek. Okay?"

"Got it," Clif said.

Adrian, Jerry, and Tim set out as Clif and Bollinger headed back. Adrian maintained the same pace as before, knowing it would only take them a day to get in sight of the raiders, since the raiders would also be moving toward them. That would leave them two days to scout, and just enough time to meet up at the barn.

They traveled all day, then set up a cold camp that

night. When Adrian took his watch, he thought about Linda. She was an attractive woman with her copper hair and blue eyes. She had a near perfect figure, slim and trim, but curved in all the right places. He shook his head. *What in hell am I thinking about? Last thing I need or want is to get involved with a woman. Alice isn't even cold in her grave yet; it's only been a bit over a year. The way she acts around me is cold and irritable, anyway. Obviously, whatever it is that I feel isn't returned. Got to stop thinking about her; too much on my plate as it is.*

With a conscious effort, Adrian wrested his thoughts away from Linda and focused on tomorrow's activities. "We'll see the raiders tomorrow, and if the setup is right, we'll hit them with a quick ambush and draw back to see how they react." He continued planning how to set up the ambush, what kind of terrain they would need, and what time of day would be best. After a little while, though, his thoughts returned to Linda. *Damn it! What's with this? I have to keep a clear mind and not get bogged down by thoughts of a woman I don't want and who doesn't want me.*

The next morning when the sun was up, they could see a plume of smoke to their east, about half a day's march. The raiders were burning another house, making them easy to find.

At midday, they were in position to see the raiders from a small rise in terrain they lay on. Adrian watched with his binoculars, careful not to let the sunlight glint off of them. He could see men leaving a burning house; it looked like it had been abandoned long ago. Adrian said to Tim and Jerry, "You know, I keep wondering why they burn every house they come to. Maybe it's so they can more or less keep track of each other. They sure don't seem to be sneaking around. It's a wonder they ever find anyone home, the way they're going about this. It doesn't make sense—it's as though they want everyone to know they're coming. It doesn't add up to a hill of beans."

MARCH 16, LATE AFTERNOON

After watching for two hours, Adrian said, "These guys don't change their habits, do they? Let's move down the line and find the middle area; maybe we can find the command group."

That afternoon, they had reached a spot where they could spy on the middle of the line, but without having spotted the command group. Adrian said, "They look like they're done for the day; they're setting up camp. Let's talk about doing a probe. I'm thinking that we wait until dark, then move in close, following that dry creek bed. First light, we open up on this group, take out a couple, and raise some general hell. Then skedaddle back to that high spot a mile southwest of here and watch to see what happens. Tim, you could set up right here and pick off a few to give us cover as we move back, then join us at that old bridge over there. We'll head for the hill together from there. What do you think?"

Tim said, "I can hit them from here, all right, as long as they aren't moving around too fast. If they get after you in a fast chase, I can slow them down, but don't count on me taking them all out for you."

Jerry said, "If you start shooting at them with that big cannon of yours, they'll think twice about chasing after us. When we get halfway to the bridge, you stop firing and move over to meet us. We should arrive at the bridge at the same time. We have two good positions before we get to the hill to fire back and slow them: that bend there and that one there," Jerry said, pointing. "But if they're really aggressive, we may be in for a long day of running."

Adrian said, "If they get too hard on our tail, Tim will head back for the barn on his own while you and I draw them off to the southwest by firing and running. You and I can outrun them, I think. I know we can lose them after we cross that other big creek; it's got thick brush on the other side. Then we'll swing around from there and meet Tim back at the barn. We've burnt one of our last two days, so all we have left is tomorrow and then we have to head back. Mostly what I want to see is how the other groups react, and maybe spot the command group."

Tim replied, "Sounds like a plan to me. I'm itching to get in a little shooting. If possible, I'll pick off their leader first. I'm pretty sure it's that tall fella."

Adrian said, "All right, then. Come dark, Jerry, and I'll work into position while you wait here. As soon as we stop shooting, you start. If you get a clean shot at the tall guy, go ahead and take it anytime after we start shooting, otherwise wait until we stop. We're only going to fire two rounds each, and then hightail it out of there. One of the worst mistakes ambushers make is hanging around too long. I know of guerrillas that only load two rounds in their magazines so they don't get too caught up in the action—it's a smart move."

Tim said, "If that fella shows me something to aim at, there won't be a nickel's worth of dog meat left of him one second later. These half-inch chunks of lead tear up a lot of territory when they hit. So start slow, that way maybe he won't take cover too fast."

MARCH 17, DAWN

Adrian and Jerry picked their main targets, but waited for four men to be open targets at the same time. It was a tense wait. Two or three would occasionally be open at a time, but not four. Adrian had begun to think that they would have to settle for two or three when suddenly, four were in the open. Four shots, sounding like one single long blast, roared from the creek bed. Four men fell. Then the tall man seemed to be picked up off his feet as a huge spray of red mist filled the air behind him. Adrian and Jerry were already on their feet and running back up the dry wash when the sound of the .50 caliber shot filled the air. By the time they had covered a hundred yards, the .50 had fired twice more, then fell silent.

Tim arrived at the bridge just seconds ahead of Adrian and Jerry. The three men ran up the dry creek bed another hundred yards and then left it to head for the hill. They made good time getting to it, using all the cover available. When they got there, Tim was exhausted. Adrian got his binoculars out and started scanning the areas he thought they might come from. As soon as he noted that Tim had caught his breath, Adrian said, "Tim, you head on to the barn now. Go in a straight line. Jerry and I will wait here until we see movement. If they're coming fast, we'll play rabbit with them and draw them away, then disappear and meet you at the barn as soon as we can. Don't shoot unless you have to. If you hear us shooting, you'll know about where we are, but keep going. Got it?"

Tim said, "Got it. See you at the barn, children." He got up and started walking without further comment.

Adrian said, "That's what I like about Tim. No nonsense, no fussing, no false heroics. He does what he says he's going to do, and does it damn well. Most men would have tried to make excuses for being slower than us, but not Tim. He just sees it as a fact and deals with it. Gotta love that, don't you?"

Jerry just grinned without taking his eyes off the distant tree line. "Look, movement at your ten."

Adrian quickly moved his field glasses to his left, following Jerry's instruction where to look. "I see four men, and they're coming fast." Swinging his glasses even farther to the left, he said, "And there are more coming from the nine position." Moving his glasses back to the right, he said, "Okay, more coming from the two spot. Looks like they're trying to make a big circle, hoping to catch us inside of it. Let's roll."

Adrian and Jerry trotted down the backside of the hill and angled off forty-five degrees to the left of Tim's line of march. They double-timed, but used all the cover they could.

MARCH 17, MORNING

After half an hour, Adrian and Jerry slowed to a walk and began looking well ahead of them. "Look over by that peach orchard, Jerry—I see eight or nine men. They're moving back in to close up the circle, and we'll be just outside of it. Once the loop is closed, I think they'll start closing the circle in, trying to flush us out.

There is definitely disciplined thought behind this; they just didn't make the circle big enough to catch us. We've got two choices: shoot some more of them, or stay silent and get back to Tim. If we start shooting, we'll likely have them on our tail all the way to the barn. I think we've found out what we can and it's best to leave them be for now. What do you think?"

Jerry replied, "Well, it's a cinch we're not going to defeat them by ourselves. What is it you always say? 'Pick battles small enough to win but big enough to count?' I agree—let's head on back."

Tim watched from the barn's roof, his .50 in the ready position as Adrian and Jerry came in. Tim watched behind them, but did not see any movement. He picked his rifle up, slung it over his shoulder, and descended the ladder. "Well, kids, I've had a nice nap and I'm ready to roll when you are. Did you have fun?"

Jerry replied, "Not a bit. Just a casual stroll through the country. We did stir them up, though."

Adrian said, "The definitely have discipline, Tim, and a plan in place for when they are attacked. They moved fast—real fast—to form a circle around where they thought we might be, and then started shrinking it. None of the scouts has mentioned that tactic at any point before this, but they moved into it fast and smooth. Their reaction had already been planned out. Makes me wonder even more about them. Things don't add up. They move cross-country in a deliberately sloppy way, then they pull a trained rapid response like that."

Tim said, "If they can pull that tactic that fast, then every damn thing else they do is deliberate, as well. That means their so-called sloppy forward advance is on purpose and planned. They have a reason for it, even though I can't quite cotton on to what that reason is. But I'll guarantee you this: they aren't total muttonheads. The only thing I can think of is they want us to know they're coming. That only makes sense to me if they think it will scare us away, and that doesn't make sense, 'cause we'd take our women with us, and you know they want women as much as they want food. Hell, maybe the sons of bitches really are just a bunch of dumbasses. I'd like to think that, but that fast circle doesn't show dumb. It shows wanting to take prisoners. It's like watching a clown suddenly turn into an acrobat, then going back to being a clown. Shit, Adrian, nothing about this makes sense to me."

Adrian replied, "Then let's use logic. They deliberately burn every house, making big smoke signals. They move slow enough, and with enough forewarning, that everyone knows they're coming miles ahead of time. They're drawing attention to that fact. So the logical conclusion is they want everyone to know they're heading toward them. The question is why?"

Jerry said, "Maybe they are trying to draw us out to them? Could they be headed to Fort Brazos for a reason and want us to come out and fight instead of forting up?"

Tim said, "Bottom line is it doesn't make any difference. We've already decided to take them on in the field, and the reasoning behind it is sound. Whether they want us to come out or not, it's still the best option. So the 'why' doesn't matter—it's what they have in mind to do once we engage that we have to think about."

Adrian said, "You're right. Meeting them in the

field is what we're going to do. Figuring out how to approach them and what their reaction will be is key. It isn't their motives we need conccrn ourselves with, it's their actions, and trying to outguess their actions is all that counts. Let's get home; I'm tired of listening to grandpa snore every night."

Tim picked up a limb and pretended he was going to give Adrian a spanking. Adrian took off running and Tim and Jerry followed at a walking pace.

CHAPTER 13

MARCH 21, EVENING

SHORTLY AFTER RETURNING TO FORT Brazos, Adrian went over the training results with Linda.

Linda reported, "We've completed all the tasks you wanted. The results are good. Surprise attacks on the village really brought out weaknesses. We've worked on those over and over. These ladies aren't going to be caught napping ever again, that's for sure. We have forward scouts out all the time now, mostly to the east, because we know that's where they're coming from, but also in all other directions in case they circle around. Even without the scouts, the women are on constant alert status. But the scouts give us a heads-up when anyone is coming. Even if the scouts get caught up, they'll have time to fire a couple of shots, and that's all the warning we need.

"The men have trained in ambushes and the specific attack tactics you suggested. The men have gotten very good at setting up ambushes, hitting hard and fast, then fading out to meet back up at a rendezvous point. We're out of paint balls and gas cylinders, but I think they've done us as much good as they're going to now anyway.

"I've identified the men and women that will be the battlefield medics and stretcher bearers. They're all in intensive training at the hospital and every one of them is catching on fast. Their morale is good, and they are all proud of their role. They are getting tremendous support from the combat teams also; they see them as battle field angels and let them know it.

"The MASH unit is organized and ready to set up wherever needed. They can set up in under twenty minutes now, excluding tents, and start moving out to relocate on a minute's notice. You didn't mention drilling them but I thought it a good idea so went ahead. They needed to learn how to pack and unpack quickly. They've also been getting training in map reading so that they can find their way to the next spot. The village hospital has been organized for rapid response to incoming patients from the MASH unit, or from walking wounded. That's something else I instituted. The medics will determine if a person can't continue to fight, but can walk to the hospital bypassing the MASH unit. If they can be treated on the battle field and returned to the fight they will be. Triage in the field, so to speak."

Adrian said, "Good report and excellent decisions. How do you feel now about being second in command?"

"Better. Your demonstrated trust in me hasn't gone unnoticed by the troops, and I was given enough rope to prove or disprove that trust. Apparently I am proving it, because I haven't had a single problem with my orders being followed. I thought I would have some trouble from the men, but I haven't."

Adrian said, "That's well and good, and as I expected,

but I meant how are you feeling yourself? What's your confidence level now?"

"As good as it can be, knowing I haven't been tested under real conditions."

"That's an honest answer. I appreciate that. I want you to know that I have one hundred percent confidence in you when the bullets are flying. I didn't choose you for this randomly, but I can't exactly explain my reasoning, because it is more of an intuitive feeling than a logical formula. My gut tells me that you'll remain cool and level no matter what, that you can and will think on your feet, and that you'll remain clear-headed and see the big picture as events change and swirl around you. That is a rare talent—staying cool and seeing the overall battlefield under intense pressure. It's what makes a leader, and exactly what the troops not only need, but fully deserve. They deserve to receive orders from someone who is in control and can act rationally and rapidly as needed.

"I'm sure you're still wondering why I didn't pick one of my own teammates from the Army to command the women. Let me add in another element I didn't go into previously. My guys are all outstanding soldiers, battle tested and excellent at what they do. What they do is follow orders extremely well. What they don't do—and never had any expectation of doing—is to have to think up what those orders should be. I was in the same boat until recently, when events forced me to take a leading role. It was sort of a field promotion. Creating battle plans, organizing troops, determining the strategy and tactics were new for me. Maybe I have some talent for it—I think I do—but more important is that other people believe I do and rely on me, so I have to do it well.

"You're in the same spot I was in. You're having this thrust on you, on top of that, you have no battle experience . I can only imagine how strange this must be for you, but I believe you have the clear-headed thinking that the role requires. A bonus is that you don't have baggage with any of the women, no old resentments from the past. The fact that you don't have battle experience, of course, creates self-doubt in your ability to carry it off. Any intelligent person would and should have those doubts. Your being a woman is not relevant; this isn't about what chromosomes you were born with, and I hope it's not playing much in your thinking. It certainly isn't in mine. If it is, just remember Joan of Arc, Zenobia, Golda Meir, Margaret Thatcher, and thousands of other female war leaders throughout history.

"It's my firm belief that you are of that quality, and it's backed up by what I've been hearing from the troops. You have my complete confidence and trust, and I feel good about you having my back. It's a solid feeling knowing you're here and that I can rely on you. Now I think it's time for you to go out on a scout and see the enemy for yourself. Choose who you want to go with you— it's your choice—and be back in short order. I'll keep the training going while you're gone."

Linda's head was reeling. She felt an involuntary surge of pride and confidence welling up from Adrian's faith in her. She suspected that was exactly what he had intended, to bolster her confidence in herself, but the feeling was undeniably heady all the same. Suddenly, she realized that she would march into Hell with a bucket of water if he asked her to. *This*, she thought to herself, *this is what a good leader does; he motivates by showing trust and respect. I'll take this as a lesson and use the same technique myself. He's proving his trust in me by sending me out on a scouting mission, choosing my own people to go with me. Damn, he's good at this.*

Linda said, "Thank you General. I promise, I will not let you down." Her smile was kept on the inside as she said it.

"Good. I don't expect you to. Now let's go over the duty roster name by name. I want to know what you think of each person."

Later that day, Matt invited Adrian and Linda to observe a test firing of his pipe cannon. "This is basically a large single shot shotgun. It can be reloaded and reused, but it takes two people half an hour to set it up again—too long for any battle I can think of. As you can see, I've set pieces of plywood downrange to get an idea of the maximum effective range as measured by spread of the chain sections. My calculations indicate that the best range will be forty yards. The cannon has rudimentary sights welded on top for horizontal alignment. Elevation is set by using this carpenter's level. At forty yards, we'll need only a few degrees of muzzle elevation for the chains to hit at a three-foot height. I've estimated the muzzle elevation at ten degrees. I'll measure where the chains actually hit and recalculate from that. Once I know for sure, the level will be marked to show the leading edge of the bubble. This test will also give me an idea of the most efficient length and number of chains to load. These are eight inches long. I love the way the chains can be rolled up and then loaded; they go in very compactly, so I can get a lot of them in there.

"Fully loaded, this thing weighs in at one hundred and sixty pounds. I'd thought I could do it under one hundred pounds, but I can't. Still, if three women shoulder this, they'll each be carrying fifty-three pounds. Put four women under it, and they'll be shouldering forty pounds. It's very portable. I've also welded lugs on each side of the barrel to tie off with. If the cannon isn't anchored, the recoil could throw the barrel back several feet. An easy way to anchor it is by doing it the way I have for this test. Two spiral anchors—like these that were used for mobile home tie downs—are screwed into the ground using a longbar for leverage, and then the cables are connected from the anchor on each side to the lug on each side. It only takes a few minutes to set the whole thing up. Sandbags, tree trunks, rock piles—almost anything can be used to rest the barrel on. But I think I have time to weld adjustable bi-pods on them like this one. Two pieces of pipe, one just small enough to slide inside the other, with holes drilled through them and a pin inserted through the holes make it easy to set these up.

"Firing it is as easy as pushing a button. Instead of using capacitors, I've used a nine-volt battery. I found some while looking for the chainsaw chains. Okay, ready to see it go boom? Stand back over there and cover your ears."

Linda and Adrian stepped away as he'd suggested. Matt followed them, stringing out wire. "I'm certain it's safe to stand right next to it, but since this is the first test fire we'll stay back out of an abundance of caution. Ready?"

Seeing the two nod, Matt pushed the igniter button. The cannon instantly roared, shaking the ground under their feet. A huge jet of orange-red flame gouted from the barrel. Blue smoke filled the air downrange, blocking their view of the plywood. The cannon rocked back against its restraints, but remained anchored. Matt did a little jig while smiling from ear to ear. "Wasn't that beautiful? Huh? Wasn't that just gorgeous?"

Adrian, a bit surprised by the violence of the cannon blast, was smiling along with Matt. Linda had a stunned look on her face. The reality of what lay ahead had just become much clearer to her.

Matt didn't wait for the smoke to clear. He took off downrange to look at the plywood panels he'd set up. Linda followed him, suddenly curious and excited. Adrian quickly followed. The damage to the plywood was unbelievable. The chain sections had ripped right through the panels. The holes were the length of the chain sections. Some were horizontal, some were vertical, and most were on an angle. The spread of the chains was forty feet. There were a few gaps between the chain strikes, but overall, if men had been standing shoulder to shoulder across that forty-foot spread, only three or four might have survived.

"Hot damn!" Matt yelled. "Hot damn! That's serious damage!" Matt almost never cursed; he was pumping with adrenaline and excitement. Linda was astonished at what she saw. Adrian was smiling now from ear to ear. "This is good stuff, Matt!"

Matt said, "I'm off to the shop to make as many of these as I can. See you kids later!" Matt turned and literally jogged back toward his shop.

Lind turned from the plywood and looked at

Adrian. She was imagining the damage this would do to humans. "Damn. I don't know what to say. This is...this is just...I don't have words for it. I'll bring the women out here and show this to them right away. It will be one hell of a morale boost for them. I'll catch up with you later." Linda took off at a fast walk back toward the village.

Adrian stood there for a long time, looking at the shredded plywood. He was beyond pleased with the cannon's effectiveness. For the first time, he began to think that the women had more than just a good chance at defending the village. They had an excellent chance if they could get enough cannons set up in the right places and used them at the right time.

MARCH 23, MIDAFTERNOON

Linda and Clif watched the two scouts that were half a mile in front of the raiders as they came directly toward them. The scouts were walking along bored and half alert, not aware that they were moving directly toward two of their enemies. Clif whispered, "If you still want to take them prisoner, they'll be here in about three minutes. We'll have to take them silently, tie their hands, gag and blindfold them, and get the hell out of here. It's that or kill them. I think we'll have about two to three hours before they're missed. Hopefully they'll be thought to have deserted, but we can't count on that. That means we'll have to move fast and not stop for anything until we're all the way back to the fort." This was a huge speech for Clif, but he liked Linda and she needed to be instructed.

Linda whispered back, "We'll take them prisoner;

they may have information we can use. I'll follow your lead on how to make the capture since you've done it before and I haven't."

Clif replied, "It's simple enough. When they are right on top of us, we stand up with our weapons cocked and ready. They'll have three choices: fight, surrender, or run. They'll know that if they fight, we have them cold and they'll die, and if they run, they'll get shot in the back before they can move two steps. The danger is that they'll react without thinking. So we stand up casually and talk casually, kind of throwing their reaction time off kilter while they try to figure out just what's happening. Worst case is they go for it, we cut them down, and we don't get two prisoners. Don't look at their eyes; watch their hands. Their eyes can't shoot you—their hands are the thing to watch. But they'll surrender, all right; we just have to make sure they do it quietly. Here they come—be ready."

Linda felt her heart pounding in her chest; she was tense all over. She controlled her breathing as she watched the pair of armed men coming closer. Finally, they were almost on top of her. Clif squeezed her arm and whispered, "Now!" and they stood up at the same time with their rifles pointed at the two men, who were now only six feet away. Linda's finger was on the trigger and she was hyper-alert to their hands, as Clif had warned her to be. The two men's eyes went wide and they started to bring their rifles to bear in a reflex motion, but froze as Clif said in a calm, matter of fact tone, "Gentlemen, you're captured or you're dead—your choice. If you make one tiny little sound, you're dead. If you twitch, you're dead.

"I want you to know we treat prisoners decently and

eventually let them go. Now, slowly bend down and place your rifles on the ground, and then slowly step over your rifles, with your hands up high." There was a moment's pause, and then Clif said, "Now. Slowly bend down and let go of the rifles." The two men paused for only a millisecond, and then one began bending down. As soon as he did, his partner followed suit. When they stood back up, their eyes shifted from Clif to Linda and back again. Linda eased her finger's pressure on the trigger a tiny fraction, but she was still tense and ready to fire.

After the two men had stepped over their rifles with their hands up, Clif patted them down and removed their side arms and knives. Clif was careful not to get between Linda's line of fire and the two men. He had them remove their shirts and quickly tore them into strips. He used the strips to bind their hands behind their backs and gag them. He made blindfolds with small slits in them and placed them over their eyes, tying them off behind their heads. "I want you men to be able to see enough to see where you're walking. Can you see?" he asked. One nodded and one shook his head no. Clif adjusted his blindfold until he could see to walk.

Clif whispered in Linda's ear, "The blindfolds are psychological. With limited vision, they are less likely to try to take off running to escape, but if they can't see at all, they'll be a constant nuisance, and we have to move fast." Linda nodded to show that she understood.

Clif then took a piece of parachute chord from his pack and tied a piece of rope from one man's waist to the other man's waist, leaving a long lead from the forward man. This was self-evident as a further means of discouraging escape attempts. The men knew they wouldn't be able to run without getting tangled in brush. Clif said, "Okay, boys, here's the drill: we're taking you to our base. I'll be in front leading you by the rope with you two following me single file. My partner will be behind you. Try anything at all, and she'll stick a knife up your ass so deep it'll cut your tonsils. Make too much noise, and you'll know you made too much noise when you feel the knife. There won't be any warning; we can travel faster with just one of you, anyway."

Clif picked up the men's weapons, the handguns and knives going into his pack and the rifles slung over his shoulder. He policed the area to make sure they had left no clues behind. The ground was hard and dry; no tracks were going to be found. Grabbing the lead end of the rope, he started off at a slow pace to give them time to adjust to walking with their new restrictions, but soon picked up the pace to a fast walk, double timing when conditions warranted it. Linda brought up the rear, her knife in hand and ready to kill quickly if need be.

They traveled the rest of the day and all that night. It was a hard, grueling walk, but stopping was out of the question. The bandits were approaching the point where Adrian would attack them, and there was no time to lose. Walking cross-country at night was difficult and slow, as there was only enough ambient light to make out shadowy shapes. The prisoners stumbled often, but they were exhausted and had shown no inclination of attempting escape. Linda and Clif exchanged places periodically, as each position had its difficulties. It helped a little.

They arrived at Fort Brazos just after dawn, exhausted, filthy, and triumphant. Bringing in prisoners had been a goal since the first scouts had gone out. These were the first ones captured, and they had been brought in undamaged. Linda was hoping that one of them held some key piece of information that Adrian would find useful. She was amazed at herself for being so eager to earn his praise, praise that she thought he had been piling on her only to keep her spirits up, not because she had earned it. Well, she had damned well earned some for these two prisoners. It made her feel good to know that she had earned this.

CHAPTER 14

MARCH 23, EVENING

REX WAS FURIOUS. THEY'D MISSED Adrian several days before. He was sure it was Adrian; the probing of the line had been coldly calculated and carried out professionally. Rex thought, *that had to be Adrian. I lost seven men—seven! All in five minutes, and not one sighting of the attackers. Bastards killed four men and ran like hell, and three more were picked off by the sniper to keep pursuit at bay. Classic, professional, perfectly executed. That was Adrian, no doubt about it. Bastard!*

Frank walked up and reported, "Two scouts missing, probably deserted. We didn't hear any shooting, no signs of bodies or even a blood trail. Probably just lit out."

Rex yelled at Frank, "YOU IDIOT! Do you really think they deserted? Where to? Why? They've been captured, and by now they're halfway back to Fort Brazos. They'll tell everything they know, which, I'll grant you, isn't much, but every little bit hurts us. Damn them for being stupid. If they come back, bring them to me, but I'm not holding my breath."

Rex turned in fury and stormed back to his tent, thinking, *if Adrian didn't know it was me coming before, he'll know tomorrow. That rat-fucking bastard won't show up out here again, not without all his men. The easy capture is out, now it's going to be me and him at some point. He'd better not get himself killed before I can get him, damn it!*

Frank said from outside the tent, "Permission to enter, sir?"

"Drag your sorry ass in here."

"Orders for tomorrow, sir?" Frank asked after ducking through the tent entry.

"Move out as usual, but double the forward scouts. They definitely know we're coming at them. If they have enough men, they'll hit us before we get there. Tell the men to expect ambushes, and not to try to encircle them anymore. Any useful information we would get now isn't worth the trouble—we know as much as we need to. Fire back to kill any ambushers, take no prisoners. Is that clear?"

"Yes sir, clear as can be. I'll pass the orders on." Frank left the tent quickly. He could see that Rex was furious, and being near a furious Rex was like hearing ice cracking under your feet.

CHAPTER 15

MARCH 25, EARLY MORNING

A DRIAN WAS ALERTED TO THE incoming scouts and prisoners by a runner. "They'll be here in twenty minutes, General."

"Thank you. You're Lindsey, aren't you?"

"Yes sir."

"Good work. I've heard good reports on you. I understand that you are one of the fastest and quietest runners we have, and better yet, your accuracy in relaying messages is top notch. We'll be relying on you heavily when the fighting starts. I want you to know I appreciate what you are doing and how critically important your role is to our success."

Lindsey's chest swelled with pride as she said, "Thank you, sir! Any more messages for me to relay?"

Adrian smiled a little and said, "Not now, carry on."

Lindsey saluted, did a perfect about-face, and took off running, her feet flying over the broken ground.

When Clif and Linda arrived with the two prisoners, Adrian had the two men separated and taken to different rooms in the house. He posted a guard on each man and had their blindfolds replaced with new ones that had no slits. He cautioned the guards to not talk to the prisoner in their charge. Once this was done, he turned to Linda and said, "Report."

Linda reported on their scouting trip and the position of the raiders. "Not much has changed, other than that they are getting close to the battlefield. They should be there in about two days, three at most."

Adrian said, "Tell me about the prisoners."

Linda replied, "We could see them coming from a mile off, and they were moving in a straight line. I thought maybe if we intercepted them, we could bring them back and see if they had any valuable information. Will you torture them? Not that I mind—just curious."

Clif smiled at the question as Adrian responded, "Torture works, but it can take a long time. With two of them, I'll play them against each other and not only get better information faster, but I'll also get corroboration, as well. Unless I miss my guess, by tonight I'll know everything they know and have it verified. They're in for a long day, but not much else. At least for now."

Linda asked, "What do you mean when you say 'at least for now?'"

Adrian looked her straight in the eye and replied, "It means that when I have all they have to offer, they'll be killed. They won't know that, of course. When they are killed, they won't know it or feel it."

Seeing the tightening of Linda's jaw, Adrian said, "It's harsh, but the reality is that prisoners will weaken us. It takes manpower to take care of them, to guard them. Even then, let's say we do keep them as prisoners: for how long? What do we do with them, turn them loose? Men who live by killing women and children? Men who rape? Should we turn them loose to continue doing that? Turn them loose on unsuspecting and innocent people? I'll tell you what, if you can come up with a better plan by morning, I'll damn sure listen to it." Adrian truly hated to kill prisoners, yet he knew it was the only valid choice. The fact that it had to be done didn't make him like it any better. Instead, it created internal conflicts that he knew he could never resolve. That is what made him jump on Linda the way he did. If she could conceive a better method of dealing with prisoners, he truly was ready to listen.

Linda smiled a grim smile and said, "Those may be the men who burned my home, would have killed my son, would have raped and then killed me. If they weren't the ones, they were certainly part of that gang of animals. No, what I was wondering was, can I be the one who kills them?"

Clif guffawed loudly and then caught himself. "She'll do, Adrian, she'll do."

Adrian was looking at Linda in a whole new light. *This is one tough woman. Rare to find one that hardcore and honest about it.* He once again began feeling the warring factions of attraction and guilt roaring through his mind. Barely able to keep his voice steady from the internal onslaught, he said, "Linda, you did a damn good job bringing in those two prisoners. When the time comes to kill them, you can certainly take part."

Linda was shocked at herself for saying out loud what she wanted to do. She wanted to kill these men, yes, but two days ago, she would never had said so, and would never have believed she could do it. Now she was aware she not only could, but it would bring her a certain satisfaction, though not pleasure. She heard Adrian's praise as though from a long distance and pulled herself together again, answering, "Thank you, General, thank you very much."

Adrian wasn't sure if she was thanking him for the praise or for allowing her to take part in killing the prisoners. He just nodded and turned to interrogating the prisoners. He no longer had any doubt that he'd chosen the right person to lead the women.

As Linda watched him walk off, she wasn't sure which she had thanked him for, either. She was still shocked by her request, and even more shocked that she had meant every word of it.

Adrian addressed the first prisoner, "In a moment, I'll remove your gag and let you have a drink of water. The blindfold and ties stay on. I'm not interested in your comfort. Then I'll begin asking you questions. You can choose to answer, and if you do so and answer truthfully, you'll be taken far out of camp, still blindfolded, in the opposite direction of your band, and released. If you're ever seen around here again, you'll be shot on sight.

"On the other hand, if you decide not to answer, then you'll be tortured until you do. I know how to torture. I know how to bring you near death just from the feeling of pain while actually keeping you quite healthy. I can stand it a hell of a lot longer than you can. It's your choice. You think about it, and I'll be back soon."

Adrian then went to the second prisoner and repeated the same instructions, then sent Clif in to question him. Adrian returned to the first prisoner. Adrian removed his gag and held a canteen to the man's mouth, letting him have two long drinks.

Adrian said, "Okay, we'll start with your name, then where you're from and how you joined this band of raiders. Then you'll tell me everything there is to know about them—how many there are, how they've trained, what their tactics are, the ultimate goal of the group, everything you know about the leader, and anything else you think I would find useful or interesting. You should realize that if you try to go back to your group, they'll know by now that you were taken prisoner and will not believe you if you tell them you didn't talk. They'll torture you to find out what you said and may have learned while here. So holding back will do you no good. Your best bet is to tell me everything, then get turned loose and hope that I use your information to kill all of them so you don't run into any of them later on down the road. Oh, and one other small thing. Your buddy has already started talking up a storm in the other room. You're behind. I'll be comparing notes on what you two are saying. Any—and I mean *any*—differences between your stories, and out come the tools. Got that?"

The first prisoner nodded and began talking, his words coming out so fast that they were tripping over each other. "My name is Gerald Franklin. I'm from Baton Rouge. I joined up with Rex's gang about a year ago. They were—"

Adrian interrupted. "Rex? Rex who?"

"Rex Gambian," Gerald replied.

Adrian felt a cold chill run down his spine like a shock wave, and he came as close to feeling fear as he was capable of. He said in a steady voice, "Continue." While the prisoner talked on, Adrian sat quietly, barely hearing him. He picked up what was said, but only in a background way. Nothing else the prisoner said was of much value, nothing his own scouts hadn't reported. As soon as he heard the name 'Rex Gambian,' Adrian knew everything he needed to know, and it was bad news.

After Gerald seemed to have run down, Adrian said, "All right. In a minute, another man will be in here and you'll start over from the beginning." Adrian left the room, shutting the door behind him. He went over to the other prisoner's room and entered. Clif had been interrogating this prisoner using the same procedure. Clif looked up at him, and Adrian could tell by his grim expression that he had already heard about Rex.

———————————

Adrian picked two men and briefed them on what the prisoners had said. "Now, go in there and make them start over and interrupt them often by picking on details. Go back and forth with the questions; don't get into a rhythm. Try to trip them up. Dig out all the details you can, take notes, and when you've wrung them out as much as you can, come see me."

Adrian told Linda, "Get all the key people to meet us at Roman's house. We have a lot to talk about."

When they were all gathered in Roman's living room, Adrian said, "Linda, you taking those prisoners was far more valuable than I would have ever imagined. You got us some extremely important information. Good work. The key information is that the raiders are led by Rex Gambian."

All of Adrian's Army buddies' faces fell at the news, all but Clif, who just continued to look grim.

"Rex? That psychotic son of a bitch? Jeeesus," Bollinger growled.

Lind asked, "Who's this Rex?"

Adrian said, "Bollinger, you tell them."

Bollinger replied, "I hate to foul my mouth with that name. He was a sergeant over in Company E. He led a group just like Adrian did, going out on the same kind of assignments. He's a stone cold psycho killer of the worst kind. The only emotion he ever showed was a violent hatred of Adrian. He was jealous of Adrian, eaten up with it, always trying to outdo him in every way. He was in constant competition with Adrian, although Adrian ignored him. He was obsessed, tried to kill Adrian once in a bar and almost succeeded. He shouldn't have been in the Army at all—too insane—but command group was willing to use that cold bastard, and I'll admit he ran very good operations. An IQ off the charts, but he's a psychotic genius killer, not someone you really want to keep around as a pet. He trained with us, knows everything we know, knows how we think and how we act and react. This is, without a doubt, the worst news we could have heard."

Adrian said, "This is all beginning to make sense now. I'm the reason they are coming straight here. I'm guessing he heard those damn stories on the ham net about me and it flared up his obsession again. The reason he has been taking his time getting here, burning everything along the way, must have been to draw me back here. Had to have been. He knew I was in Colorado, and that it would take time for word to get to me and then for me to come back. He's not coming here for the food and women; he's coming here for me. He is definitely that crazy. That man hates me with every molecule in his body. He probably told his men they were coming to a land of plenty, ripe and easy pickings. He's kept them half-starved and made sure everyone in the countryside was willing to kill them. It's kept the men in line; they'd be too scared to desert, knowing how everyone in the countryside feels about them. Now that they are almost here, it's do or die for them. If they don't take this village, they'll starve to death, and they know it. It's classic psychopathic manipulation."

Adrian said, "If there was a way to get him one on one, I'd do it in a heartbeat."

John replied, "Won't happen. He knows that you would kill him, so he won't let it happen that way. He wants you dead, but he wants to be alive afterwards, too. Besides, even if you removed him, we would still have to deal with his men; they will likely starve if they don't take the village, and they know it."

Bollinger said, "With Rex in the lead, we can pretty well guess what he'll do, how he'll move his men around."

Adrian replied, "We'll know what he will do, but he will know what we will do, too. It's like a chess match: trying to outguess the opponents moves several steps ahead based on what they know of each other's game style. We can throw some surprises at each other, but how many and how effective?

"We have different strengths and weaknesses. His strengths are that his men have fought and maneuvered together for a long time, they have to take the village or starve, and they have no base that has to be defended.

His weaknesses are that his men are hungry and maybe a little weak from that, their ammunition supply probably can't sustain a lengthy battle, and his men's motivation may not stop desertions when they find out it's going to be a hard, brutal fight they don't have much chance of winning. They won't be used to the kind of fighting they're about to see. I doubt they've ever been up against anything remotely like what we're about to throw at them.

"Our weaknesses are that our men haven't had enough training, haven't fought in a pitched battle, don't have all that much more ammunition, and haven't worked together before. Our strengths, on the other hand, are formidable. We are fighting for our family's survival, we are well fed and strong, we have trained as realistically as possible and are well organized. Plus our men, while not exactly battle hardened, are all grid survivors and tough as nails. Not many weaklings survived this long after the grid.

"I'd say that on the field it's a pretty even match, except for their numbers. We have to overcome their numbers and their other strengths by being faster and more effective than they are. Simply put, we can win if we strike hard and fast and out of nowhere.

Roman said, "Get the ambush team moving before daylight. I want you to start hitting them as soon as you can; small, quick strikes, then fade back, regroup, and hit again somewhere else. Put those bastards in a bind. Your job is to slow them down, keep them busy, and to kill as many as you can in the process, but the primary goal remains slowing them down. Linda, begin the process of evacuating the villagers to the secondary location. Clif, notify the main assault force to be ready to move out at noon tomorrow. Get extra scouts moving out tonight, I want position reports as fast and as often as you can get them. We should be in position to hit them hard in two days, on our terms and on our choice of terrain."

Before dark that evening, Linda and Clif tied the two prisoners together as before and led them north from the village. After traveling a mile Clif gave Linda the nod and they quietly pulled their pistols. Clif told the men, "Ok, this is where we release you. When the blindfolds are off, just keep going the direction you're facing until you are a hell of a long way from here, then you can untie yourselves." With that, Clif put his pistol just behind his prisoner's head, and Linda, seeing what he was doing, did the same. Clif fired, and Linda fired a split second later. The two bodies crumpled straight down without a twitch.

Clif gave Linda a long, searching look. Seeing no sign of remorse or guilt in her face, he said, "Let's head back."

Linda followed him back to the village. She was amazed at how she felt. It was as though she had done nothing more than shoot a snake in the garden.

CHAPTER 16

MARCH 26, NOON

ADRIAN STOOD BEFORE THE ASSEMBLED men. He looked them over, noting they appeared eager to get on with the fight, as they should be. They were facing not only a threat to their lives, but to their families, their homes and their hard won crops; and they had been training hard. Good training made men eager to fight, to test what they had learned, and themselves. This was a hard looking bunch, reminding him of what the early American militias must have looked like. Each man dressed according to his own taste, weapons of all kinds and makes, mostly they were bearded and skinny from the daily work of surviving by their own hands for years. They were fiercely independent individuals that had come together to face a common threat. These men were the new salt of the American nation, its new backbone. These men, these pioneers, he now believed would fight fiercely and well.

Adrian raised his voice to be heard all the way to the back. "Men, this will be the last time I'll be able to gather you together in a bunch and shout. From here on, orders will come to you by chain of command, quietly and while we are trying to stay invisible to the enemy. So I'll take this occasion to make a short speech.

"Patton said, 'No bastard ever won a war by dying for his country. He won it by making the other poor dumb bastard die for his country.' Remember that as we face a vicious enemy willing to die to take our village, to rape our women and our children, and then kill them. That is their goal, their desire, their driving need. They will do this if it kills them, and it's our job to kill them. They have us outnumbered, but we have them outclassed. We *will* kill them before they can get here! We will do it by attacking them in the field, and attacking with a fierceness they have never encountered in their lives, or dreamed of in their worst nightmares. Your job is to kill them, not to get killed yourself.

"We will take losses, that's a fact. If we stick to discipline and training, we will minimize our losses to the maximum extent possible. But even under the best of circumstances, some of you will die on this campaign. I will not come back alive if we lose. You need to have a clear picture of this in your minds. We are going to fight to the last stand, to the last bullet, to the last man. I don't believe it will come to that, but each of you has to be prepared for it in your own heart. This is your last chance; if you aren't willing to die for your family and friends, then you need to stay behind. If you're not willing to lay down your life, you could do us more harm than good, and I would rather not have you with us. If you can't make that commitment, simply stay behind when we march, or fall back at any time along the way before the shooting starts.

"I also want every man to know this: if you die, after we win, your family will be taken care of. We will see to it that they have everything they need. They will not be abandoned after your sacrifice; they will want for nothing.

"We attack day after tomorrow at dawn. The ambush team has already left to begin killing, harassing, and slowing them down for us."

The men looked back at Adrian with a solemnity that spoke of their determination. Adrian didn't believe a single man would stay behind or return before the fighting started, but he had to make it clear they could.

The men remained silent. Many looking down, some were looking around at the other men, wondering who wouldn't come back. All of them were wondering if they would be coming back. Most of the men were looking at Adrian. There were no jokes about speeches or bear cubs this time.

Adrian waited a long moment and then shouted, "Let's move out!"

MARCH 27, EARLY MORNING

Perry, Matthew, Roman, and Tim were the guerilla team and were already in position to watch the raiders. They were older and slower on foot than the main body, but they were also intelligent, experienced, and more than willing. The four men had been watching one of the raider groups since the sun had come up. Perry was, by unstated consent, leading the team. These four men had known each other for decades and knew each other well. They had many common bonds, not the least of which was they were all military veterans.

Each had different strengths and talents, and each was primarily a lone wolf. They let Perry lead because of his unusual ability to out think any of the other three on just about any topic. A tough act with these men.

Perry said, "Okay, they'll be crossing the meadow in about half an hour. Tim, you set up here with your fifty-cal and take out the lead man. Matt, you move to that small grove of trees to be closer. Roman, you take position behind that pile of boulders. I'll be in that draw just over there; we'll have them in a neat crossfire. I'll take the number two man as soon as Tim shoots, and Matt will take the number three guy, and Roman the fourth man. Tim, you take the shot when they are halfway across the meadow. That will put them in our range.

"That's all we are here to do for now—one shot each, two at the most. Tim, you'll cover us with one more shots if needed. Take out whoever you can and make them hunker for a few minutes. We leave immediately and spread out, meeting up as soon as we can at the old windmill. From there, we go into watch mode, figure out our next ambush spot. Any questions?"

Tim asked, "Why not take a few more? We've got the room for it, and there'll be several exposed."

Perry replied, "Because that's not the mission. The mission is to hit fast and run fast, you old codger, and you can't run fast."

"So you're saying if I could run faster, we could kill more?"

"No, not really. I was just poking at you for a reaction. Fact is that staying too long at an ambush is a tactical error. Adrian explained it some, and he's right. Our mission is to slow them down, make them timid about moving forward. Killing some of them is the means to that end. Killing more than four or five does not slow them down any more than killing six or seven would. We could sit here and kill eight or even ten, but then they have a much better chance of getting one or more of us because we stayed too long. On the other hand, by killing four or five and getting away, we can do it again and again. In the long run, we'll kill more of them by not getting too greedy. Pigs get fat, but hogs get slaughtered, you know. We want to be pigs, not hogs. The more often we can hit them in different places, the more timid they'll all become, and that definitely enhances our mission. One or two hits will make them timid. Ten or fifteen hits spread all over the place will make them downright scared to move. Our job is to hit them and survive, and hit them and survive, over and over and over."

"Yeah, I know, it's just like you said: I get greedy. Okay, I'll do it your way," Tim said with a wink.

Roman jumped in, "Are you sure it's hogs that get slaughtered? I always thought it was the other way around. I'm not much in favor of being called a pig."

Perry, realizing he'd been subtly poked back by Tim and knowing that Roman liked to make irrelevant statements in a crisis just to see the reactions, his sense of humor being somewhat strange, smiled ruefully and said, "All right, then, let's go."

Forty minutes later, the raider in the lead seemed to briefly levitate in the middle of the meadow. Perry knew it wasn't the hard hit from the fifty-caliber bullet; it was the man's final reflex action of his life, the bullet must have torn his spine out sending one massive spasm signal to the muscles. As the raider crumbled to the ground a spray of blood covered the man behind him and simultaneously, the sound of the fifty-caliber sniper rifle boomed in the distance. Perry had his bead drawn on the second man already, as Matt had on the third man and Roman on the fourth. Within a half-second of the lead man dropping, Perry, Matt, and Roman fired simultaneously. Three more men dropped—less dramatically, but just as dead.

Perry took off. He had taken only a few steps when he heard the roar of the fifty-caliber again and knew another raider was down. He did not turn to look or slow down. All four men took diverging paths, and quickly melted into the woods. Their rendezvous had been chosen carefully. It was easy to find, southwest of the raider's line so that if they tried the circling maneuver, they would be outside the circle. It was far enough away to be out of the raiders' immediate reach, but close enough for them to get to without exhausting themselves.

Tim arrived first and set up immediately to provide cover fire if need be. Within half an hour, Perry came in. Tim spotted him from a distance, losing sight of him most of the time as Perry used the terrain for cover. Ten minutes later, Matt came in and five minutes after that Roman joined them.

Perry said, "Five down, and they'll be considerably slower moving forward. Now, let's look at the map and pick our next attack. We have time for more ambushes before Adrian hits them, then our job changes to flank support. I'm thinking we can do more damage if we split up and hit them individually."

Matt said, "I like that idea. We can spread out and operate on our own. Pop up here and there, hit fast, and then drift off and do it again. I like it. When do we start?"

Tim said, "First thing tomorrow."

Roman chimed in, "Good, I'm getting tired of taking care of you guys."

Perry laughed. "I guess we are in accord, then. Okay, let's get together every night and compare notes. I'll take the north end of their line. Tim, you and Roman take each side of center, and Matt the south end. Choose your spots as they present themselves to you. With luck, we may be able to each hit them two or three times tomorrow. That should keep them sticking in tight cover and moving slow. I still think it best if we each go for one or two kills max in these solo ambushes. Tim might take up to three if he has enough range on them. We can meet up tomorrow evening at the little waterfall on Mill's Creek." Perry showed them the spot on the map; he had been fishing there before.

By dawn the next morning, Matt had gotten into position. He easily found the raider's camp by their campfires. The raiders still seemed bent on being obvious. As the light increased, he saw two scouts moving towards him. They were walking along an old fence line, staying in the cover of the brush and trees that had grown up next to it.

Matt thought about how that would work out when he started shooting. These two men could come around behind him if he waited much longer. *On the other hand*, he thought, *why not take them out? That would be twice as effective because I would also be putting their eyes out.* With that, Matt eased back from his chosen ambush spot, and using terrain and tree cover, moved into a spot up the fence line, took cover, and waited.

He had noted that the two scouts stayed side by side as they walked and this gave him another idea. He'd been carrying one of his modified shotguns strapped over his back. Why not wait until they are close then take them both? With that in mind, he placed his M4 on the ground next to him and took the shotgun off the sling. He lay back down and waited.

Forty-five minutes later, he could hear them coming. The fools were occasionally talking to each other and not whispering. They were bitching about being singled out for scout duty; neither appreciated being away from the main group. Within a couple of minutes, he could see them coming towards him, they were still walking only a couple of feet apart. They were moving slowly and looking around with focused attention. Since the shotgun only had two shots before reloading Matt decided that when he fired the second shot, he would drop down and grab the M4 and pop back up shooting again, if need be.

When the two men were twenty yards away, Matt popped up, shotgun at his shoulder. He came up with the shotgun already aimed at the man on the right and he fired, moving his finger to the rear trigger as he swung left, and when he was centered on the man's chest, he fired again. Both men were virtually blown apart in just over a second. He reloaded, shouldered the shotgun on its strap and picked up his M4. Then he walked up to the two bodies. The amount of carnage the .779 saboted slugs had wreaked upon the two men was extreme. Both men were hit center mass. The entry wounds were the size of the slug, but the exit wounds were almost as big around as a pie plate. The massive slug had penetrated and then mushroomed, just as designed. Matt looked around and then moved back up the fence line quickly. He had plenty of time for two more assaults on the raiders. In the distance, he heard the booming voice of Tim's fifty-caliber. Then two more booms two seconds apart. *Tim doesn't miss—he nailed three more in a bit over three seconds. Damn glad he's on our side.*

Tim lay down beside his rifle. He had dug the bipod's legs slightly into the ground so there would be no wobble after the first shot. The scope made the men look as though they were only a few feet away. The way it gathered in light made the early dawn seem to be high noon. "Range just over nine-hundred yards, no wind, simple shot." He had set the cross hairs for a dead on aim point for the distance. "Best bet is to wait until two or three of them are lined up, take the closest one, then move the sight up a hair and take the second one. Might get a third if he doesn't drop behind cover too quickly."

Matt waited what seemed like hours for three men to move into a line with each other. He heard distant twin booms, almost simultaneous shots. *Damn, I bet Matt is playing with his shotgun, nothing else sounds like that meat eater.* Matt smiled while watching through his scope, the distant gunfire had made the raiders visibly nervous. Two minutes later he had his three men lined up. As soon as he did he fired the first shot and recovered his sight profile after the resulting movement from the recoil. He then moved the sights up a hair onto the second man and squeezed the trigger. As soon as he recovered the sight picture again the third man had moved forward directly into the aim spot and Tim fired a third time.

The first man had gone down, stunning the second man into a second of immobility as he watched the man's back blow towards him. Before he could react he was hit in the chest with a sledgehammer blow and went down. The third man reacted by darting forward, trying to get to a downed tree, but just as he was diving for the cover, he was slammed down. Everyone else in the group behind them disappeared as they took cover.

Tim watched for a couple of minutes. *Between me and Matt, that's five; I wonder what Perry and Roman are up to?* He didn't consider that Matt shot twice at one man, or that he may have missed, Matt didn't miss. No one from the raider group was coming in pursuit. With slow movements, he eased back into cover and walked off.

Perry watched a group of the raiders eating breakfast. *Scurvy bunch of assholes*, he thought while he waited. He had chosen his spot carefully, based primarily on advantageous terrain. Once again, he was using a dry creek bed. The bottom of the bed was sand. Without getting down into the creek bed, he had walked alongside it, looking for two easy places to enter or exit the steep banks. He needed one close to the raiders and one much farther back, and both had to be on the opposite side of the creek from the raiders.

When he had the two spots identified, he entered the creek bed at the location closest to the raiders. Then, facing away from them, he ran up the creek bed to the second exit location he had chosen, and up and out of the creek. Then he went back to the first spot and re-entered the creek, being careful to walk along the edges where he wouldn't leave footprints. Perry took up his sniping spot. He was in a standing position with the creek bank at just the right height to support his rifle. He had a good field of fire, and a quick exit point on the far side of the creek from the raiders with extensive tree and brush cover. He could fire, disappear over the creek bank into heavy trees, and then head for his next ambush spot.

It was only a matter of seconds before he acquired his targets and began shooting. Perry rapidly fired two times, dropping two men before the rest of the men could scramble for cover. Perry then ran in the middle of the creek to his exit point, the one closest to the raiders. He carefully made his footprints in the sand line up with the footprints he had left earlier, the ones that led to the other exit point. Unless they had a skilled tracker with them, they would follow his tracks all the way up the creek. When he had accomplished that, he exited the creek bank and disappeared into the woods.

When the raiders pursued, they would keep going past where he had actually exited and then well up the creek. *Let's see if they come out of the creek bed with a paddle. I'll have a new name to put on the map for this creek if they don't.* He mused as he jogged toward his second ambush point. The false exit spot would be another prime ambush spot. He knew exactly where they would come out of the creek and he had just enough time to set up. After two or three came over the bank, he would cut them down, then he would disappear again. Perry smiled as he moved through the woods.

Roman had been watching the way the different groups set up their camps, each separated from the other by several hundred yards. This gave him an idea, a somewhat high-risk idea, but one that had an undeniable appeal to him. Using their campfires to spot them, he slowly and carefully eased his way between two campsites in the dark. He watched for sentries, but doubted they would be alert this time of night—if there even were any. By dawn, he was behind the raiders' line.

His idea was to confuse the raiders by attacking from a completely different direction to make them start watching their back trail instead of assuming no one was behind them. If anything would slow them down, it would be having to watch behind them as well as in front. It only took him a half hour to locate a good ambush spot. A heavy cove of trees that extended along an ancient fence line led back into a boggy area. It gave him cover to retreat, then circle back and find his way through their lines to get in front of them again. That was the dangerous part, moving through them in daylight.

He decided that if he couldn't get back through he would simply stay behind them and skip the nightly rendezvous, operating on his own until the big battle. The others might worry when he didn't show up, but worrying that others were worried wasn't something to be taken into account during a war. He liked the plan—he liked it a lot.

Just as the men he was watching finished packing up and starting to move out, Roman fired two times, dropping two men. He then evacuated the area using the tree line. When he got to the bog, he circled around it and followed a dry wash to another heavily forested area and started moving back toward the raiders again. When he achieved a visual on another of their groups, he could tell he wasn't going to the rendezvous that night. They were stirred up like a kicked-over fire ant nest; his and his compadres' ambushes were definitely working. Instead of trying to slip through, he eased in closer and shot two more, then quickly moved back. *Hell, I can keep this up as long as I have ammo, and I have plenty of,* he thought as he began circling back for another shot or two. Roman was enjoying having the entire backfield to himself. *It gives me a lot more latitude. No pun intended."* He thought.

That evening Perry, Tim, and Matt rejoined by the little waterfall. Once they were together, they sat down to eat the cold ration bars that Sarah's team had put together. They weren't very tasty, but they packed a big calorie load and served their purpose.

Tim was the first to comment on Roman's absence. "I hope he got lost again, I'd hate like hell if he got killed. He never did have a good sense of direction. Damned old fool could get lost in a phone booth."

Matt replied, "I heard shooting from back behind their lines; I wouldn't be surprised if he didn't wander right through them in the dark and found himself stuck back there behind them."

Tim added, "I've seen him get lost in San Angelo, of all places, and more than once. Simple little town like that, and he'd get lost like he was down in the fucking Amazon Basin without a compass. I'm with Matt—I thought I heard gunfire behind them and was thinking it had to be that damn Roman; who else could be back there? Hells bells, who else *would* be back there but him? It's just the sort of stunt he likes to pull. If he's smart, he'll stay back there and keep hitting them from behind. Pretty good idea, too, making them watch their six as well as their twelve. He better be back there, dammit, or I'll beat the shit out of him when he shows up."

MARCH 27, EARLY EVENING

Adrian sat on the ground with a map across his lap. He had just received the latest scout reports and sent the scouts back out. He pointed at a spot on the map that showed two hills near each other.

Adrian said, "Bollinger, let's go over the plan again. We're going to use these two hills and the draw between them. Rex's men are east of them a mile or so right now. He's pulled his men in a bit closer together, thanks to the ambush team, but they are still too spread out to suit this operation. I've gone over every strategy and tactic that I can think of, knowing Rex knows all of them, too. I'm hoping that he is expecting us to do something fancy and tricky—that's usually the way his mind works. So we're going to do something simple and as old as war itself.

"We're going to use Sioux battle tactics. Hit them with a small force, engage them, and then suddenly run in panic to get them to give chase into our real ambush. The trick is to not give them time to think about it, so the attack will be close to the ambush spot, maybe two hundred yards. I'll lead the hit team and then pull back through the draw between these two hills. Our main body will be split into four groups, one on each hill, one right here on the west end of the draw, and the fourth, led by you, will be hidden on the east side of the north hill. As soon as the last of Rex's men passes by, you move in behind them and plug the rear of the draw. We'll have them surrounded with two of those positions, having the advantage of height. From there, it stays just as simple: everyone fires at their own discretion, picking them off.

"Rex will have two options: stand and fight, which I doubt; or gather his men close and charge one of the groups to try and overrun them and get out of the ambush zone. I don't think he will try to take the hills—the terrain works against him too much. So it's either charge backwards or charge forward. My guess is, knowing Rex, that he'll charge forward. He never liked to back up, and going forward puts him closer to the village. If he can break through, he knows it will be to his advantage to get between us and the village. Based on that I'm going to have most of the men on the west end of the draw. I'll be joining up with them as we pull back. You'll be in position against their rear and the men on the hills will have a clear field of fire without worry of crossfire. The two teams on the ends of the draw will have to be careful or we could end up shooting into each other. Make sure everyone knows to take specific aim at an enemy only, no wild shooting.

"My group will be entrenched and take advantage of cover. Rex will have to keep moving, which exposes his men. You'll direct the other three groups, joining them up and tackling the rear. Your men will have to be moving which exposes you, but you'll be getting a little less heat if Rex keeps his men moving forward. What do you think? What are the weaknesses?"

Bollinger replied, "The first weakness is that they might not chase you. It's so old of a trick that only a greenhorn would fall for it. Rex won't, unless he is overthinking and suspecting that you actually want him to not follow, that you're double-bluffing him. I think he might just do that—overthink it, I mean. He'll be thinking that you have something up your sleeve and that by not following he'll be in a weak spot; that you want him to stay where he is or move right or left. I think you might need to help him along with that thought a bit, have some of the scouts flash a light at them from their rear and flanks a couple of times before daybreak—nothing obvious, just a few flashes to let them know someone is out there. Do that before you attack to give him time to spin his mind up tight trying to out think what you're doing. He'll be expecting tricks, because, like you said, that's how his mind works. Sometimes being as smart as he is turns into a handicap.

"The other weakness is that he moves forward, but on a tangent going either north or south of the hills, and gets around us. The only defense against that is to have the men ready for it and have a plan in place to move into his line of march and engage."

Adrian replied, "I like the flashlights, ask for volunteers. Make it clear that this is only a ploy, no engagement with them, it won't do anything except weaken our ploy, make real sure they understand that because these men are eager to start shooting. Also, pull the guerilla groups into a position to fire on the raiders if they choose one of the tangents instead of the draw. They can buy us time to bring the other men into position. If the raiders don't go on a tangent, the guerillas can come in and join your group in the east."

Bollinger said, "Done."

MARCH 27, LATE EVENING

Linda gathered the women fighters together. They were sitting near the eastern edge of the village defense line.

Linda said, "Our mission is to defend the village

as a last straw defense. A Hail Mary kind of defense. Everyone else has been evacuated; it's just us here now. The reason that Adrian didn't take us on the battlefield is because he was worried that the men would become overprotective of us, and therefore less effective. It's a good reason, a sound reason. But it has flaws. First flaw is that we are only defending property. I know it's important to defend our homes and crops and livestock, but is it critically important? If we save all this but lose our men in the process, can we call that victory? Would we want to live on like that? You tell me."

While the women were looking at Linda and shaking their heads back and forth Shirley asked, "What are you suggesting we do instead?"

Linda replied, "I'm suggesting that we follow the men out onto the battlefield, stay together as a unit, and provide them with backup reinforcement. I'm suggesting that we get into a position behind them where we can see what's happening and move into any area that needs to be supported. I'm fully aware that we may startle the men, and maybe some of them will be distracted when we arrive. But our bullets kill the same as their bullets, and if they need support, I'm confident we can provide it. However, it's also necessary that those that go are willing to go, want to go, and believe it's the best thing to do. Sitting here on our hands doesn't appeal to me.

"The options for you to consider are to go with me, stay here to defend our houses, or pull all the way back to defend the older people and children at the evacuation point. Personally, I think it would be best for any that don't want to go with me to pull back and defend the evacuation point. If the raiders get past the men—and us—they may eventually find the evacuees, so they will have to move as far away as they can as fast as they can and you can certainly be a positive help with that. Bottom line is that I am going to the battlefield—alone, if need be.

"Now, those who want to provide protection at the evacuation point, raise your hands." Four women slowly raised their hands. Linda continued, "Those who want to go with me, raise yours." The rest of the women quickly raised their hands.

Linda said, "We've got a few hours of daylight left. Go home, get your gear, and meet me here in thirty minutes. Bring four of Matt's cannons; we'll take turns carrying them in teams of three. We'll be marching all night. I know where Adrian plans the first engagement, and we have just enough time to get there before the shooting starts. We're burning daylight, ladies, let's move!"

CHAPTER 17

MARCH 27, MORNING

"FRANK, BRING IN THE GROUP leaders, we're going to have a council of war."

Frank left and sent runners out to bring the men in. Within two hours, they were gathered.

"We've been hit by nine ambushes in the last twenty-four hours. We're about two days of hard marching from Fort Brazos. My gut tells me that we will engage the enemy in a major battle sometime tomorrow or the next day, probably tomorrow. They'll throw every man they have against us, trying to defeat us before you can get to their women.

"These are farmers, not soldiers. They may have a few soldiers among them, but the majority of them are farmers. Their tactics have been to hit and run so far, not a very brave way to fight—about what you might expect from untrained hicks. The battle we come against tomorrow will be the one that breaks their back. They'll hit us and we'll hit back twice as hard. Your job is to kill as many of them as you can before they run. The more of them you kill out here, the fewer of them you'll have to chase from house to house later.

"I expect strict discipline. Follow your orders and you'll win. It's that simple. Return to your groups and first thing tomorrow morning every group draw in tight to the center. We'll no longer be using a stretched out line, now we'll continue as a single group. Frank, you line them out for tomorrow as to what position each group will take. Dismissed!"

CHAPTER 18

MARCH 28, PRE DAWN

L INDA'S TEAM, TIRED FROM THE long night march, arrived at the point where she had intended. They had barely sat down to rest when one of the Adrian's scouts walked into their camp.

He said, "What the hell are you women doing here? You're supposed to be back at the village."

Linda replied, "Go tell Adrian we are here right behind him, and intend to help if we can. We'll remain here until we see how the battle develops, then jump in at any weak spot if we are needed. Tell him we're not going back."

The scout growled an obscenity, and then silently disappeared back into the dark.

Adrian shook his head at the scout's report. "Damn it, we're attacking in just a few minutes. There's no time to go back and argue with them. Look, you go back and tell them to pull back to the village. Tell Colonel Fremont I said that's an order."

Adrian turned to Bollinger and said, "You ever hear of such a thing? Shit. I hope they don't get involved in this. We're going ahead with our plan. We're going to have enough trouble with the weather without worrying about them. If this rain gets heavy, we're going to have limited visual contact. Get the men saddled up; we're moving out in five minutes."

Adrian's group of ten men moved swiftly through the draw. Daylight would be breaking in a few minutes, but the light would be subdued by the heavy cloud cover and the light rain that was falling sporadically. A huge thunderstorm was moving in rapidly from the southwest. The booming thunder was coming closer and the lightning was nearly constant. Adrian was worried about continuing this operation with the storm rapidly approaching, and thought briefly of pulling back and waiting out the storm, but he was aware that it would be as much hindrance for Rex's men as it would be for his. It could also give Rex cover to move his men. Under cover of heavy rain, they could disappear and be hell to find and fight without the right terrain.

When they got within a hundred yards of the raiders' line Adrian said in a voice too soft to carry beyond his men, "Remember, our mission is to draw them together and then to run like hell, getting them to chase us. We're going to open fire in a minute—this is one of the few times I don't want you to carefully pick your targets. I want you to lay down a steady barrage of fire, moving back and forth frequently to make it look like there are more of us than just eleven men. We want them to think this is the main body, and that means faking them out to believe there are a lot more of us right here. Now, spread out in a line with thirty feet intervals between you, five to each side of me. When I fire, start firing, fire three or four shots, move over a few feet fire, and move back, and keep repeating until we fall back. Keep your heads down, just point and shoot. Okay, spread out."

MARCH 28, DAWN

Adrian waited patiently for the light to improve. He watched the storm coming closer and hoped it would veer off or break up, but it didn't look like it would. He guessed they had maybe a half-hour before it was on top of them. He had already sent his orders to all the groups to continue the operation through the storm.

Adrian sighted on a raider and squeezed off a shot, thinking, *might as well make the first shot count.* Then he began shooting rapidly. With his first shot, the ten men in his group opened up. It was an impressive barrage of bullets flying into the raiders. The men fired, shifted, fired again. From the raiders' perspective, it would seem that they were being attacked by at least thirty men. The raiders quickly took cover and began sporadically firing back. The sound of rifles could easily be heard above the rolling thunder of the storm. The storm's wind front hit at the same time, wind gusts struck like a hurricane, bending and whipping trees, tearing off tree limbs, debris flying through the air. It was a wild scene: men shooting and shouting, wind blowing, thunder rumbling and lightning flashing, muzzle flashes, screams of agony and rage as the sun gradually gained in height. The air turned cold as the wind surge died down. Adrian's men were keeping up a steady stream of fire through it all.

The raiders were pulling into a tight center, Rex apparently falling for the bait, as well as recognizing that the storm would cause communication problems if his men were strung out and groups of them might wander into each other. They were firing back, their firing getting heavier as they settled into a line.

Adrian signaled for his men to slow down the fire, as though they might be running low on ammunition, then he slowed it down more. Then during a flash of lightning he saw Rex's men slowly moving forward. Adrian gave his men the signal to run, stopping only occasionally to turn and fire back. As they began their retreat into the draw Rex's men boiled out of the trees running, their bloodlust stirred up at the sight of the retreating enemy. Adrian could see that Rex had lost control of his men—at least temporarily—as they charged headlong at high speed. The trap was working, as it had thousands of times throughout history. It played on a particular primal instinct, the same instinct that all predators had: charge and attack at the sight of a weak prey fleeing.

Adrian was behind his men, closest to the enemy. He directed the men to keep moving and to zig and zag, picking up speed as they gained the midpoint between the hills. He stopped and fired back at the raiders, noting that they were gaining quickly and that they were strung out with the best runners out front. *Perfect*, he thought to himself, *absolutely perfect*. He turned to run again and saw one of his men take a hit. Adrian caught up to him and saw he had been hit in the leg. He picked the man up and continued to run. Adrian was so full of adrenaline that the man felt like he weighed no more than a child.

MARCH 28, EARLY MORNING

Linda tried to watch the battle unfold. The scout had returned with orders from Adrian to return to the village, but she wasn't about to. Once the scout was convinced that the women weren't going back he explained the battle tactics and the men's locations. Linda understood the setup clearly; what she couldn't do was see it clearly in the dim light and the increasing rain. The coming storm looked to be a bad one. She knew this could be either a blessing or a curse, but at this point, she didn't know which one.

She drew Shirley to her side and said, "This storm changes everything. We can't see what's happening clearly enough. If we go in to help now, we could really screw things up. I hate sitting here and waiting as much as I hated sitting in the village and waiting. But right now, it's the only thing to do. Spread the women out in a skirmish line. Set the pipe cannons up along the line and for God's sake don't forget to tie them down with the auger anchors or they'll take off behind us like a rocket. Cut some material and stuff it in the cannons' mouths to keep rain water out of them. Make sure the women remember to not get behind them when they're fired. Set the elevation for hitting out at forty yards, just like we practiced. Tell them that we're in a tricky situation. If we see men coming at us, they will probably be our own men, so no shooting unless there is positive identification of raiders. That means no shooting unless the men are right on top of us and we are absolutely certain they're not ours. By the time we can shoot it's going to be extremely close range. The other problem is that Adrian may not have had time to get the word to all of our men that we are out here. There's a possibility that they'll shoot at us until they recognize who we are. It's dicey, but it can be controlled as long as we all keep our heads. Explain it to them so they clearly understand the situation. Spread them out, but not too far."

Shirley left to relay the orders. Linda was alone with her thoughts when she heard the shooting start. The sound of the rifles was almost swept away when the high winds burst through, but soon came back as the storms front edge moved on. From her position, she could occasionally see the men falling back when lightning lit the sky up. The lightning wasn't frequent enough to get a solid visual on the field, though as the storm came closer, the lightning was more frequent and brighter. Rain began to fall more heavily.

Adrian joined up with his main group on the western end of the draw. Now it was a matter of waiting for Rex's men to fill the draw between the hills and for Clif to close the east end. This could be a long day of battle as his men sniped off Rex's men. If they could keep Rex contained in the draw, it would end here.

Bollinger waited and watched. Rex's men were still streaming into the draw. He would either wait until he saw no more men coming, or until he saw Rex's men coming back out of the draw before he moved his men into position. At this range, he could make them out clearly during the lightning flashes, although the increasing rain was beginning to make that more difficult. Bollinger had not seen a raider for the past sixty seconds—time to close the hole. He waved his men into position.

MARCH 28, EARLY MORNING

Adrian chose a target, fired, and watched the man fall. He could see muzzle flashes all around the raiders, and the raiders firing back. Adrian heard a distant roaring sound. The sound was coming closer, sounding like a giant freight train. He looked to the southwest and saw it, a funnel cloud reaching to the earth, visible only when backlit by lightning. Hail began falling, small pellets at first, but swiftly growing to a crescendo of golf ball-sized missiles.

Shit! Adrian thought. He called out to the men, "Hang tight! They're getting hit, too. Watch and wait for a good shot, then take it. Hold your positions. Spread the word!" Adrian knew that hailstorms were usually brief and hoped this one would be. The approaching tornado was a greater threat than Rex at the moment; it seemed to be heading straight for them, but there was absolutely nothing that could be done about it. He watched with growing anxiety as it roared toward them.

The wind was gaining strength by the second, trees now seeming to bend and stretch at their roots, leaves stripping off and flying away like great gusts of smoke. The hail stopped and the wind gained even more strength, then with an increased roar the tornado was almost on them. It passed by just east of the two hills, where the battle was still raggedly unfolding. The world went almost black, interrupted by frequent close-by lightning strikes and booming thunder. As it reached a crescendo Adrian saw trees swirling up and around the tornado's cone not a quarter of a mile away. The tornado paused, seemed to head towards the battle for a second, hesitated again, and turned back to its original path, just missing the battle zone, and then the rain fell so hard that visibility was limited to a few feet. There was no sound of gunfire now; no one could see far enough to shoot. The rain was ice cold.

The roar of the tornado gradually lessened as it continued cutting its way to the northeast. Rain was still falling heavily, but beginning to diminish. Adrian knew from experience that these kinds of storms moved fast and the rain would likely be done in only minutes. He waited, watching steam coming from the ground from the cold rain hitting the warm earth, steam that was ripped to shreds by the rain and wind. It would only be a matter of minutes now. He hoped against hope that Rex's men hadn't gained some advantage from the storm. He yelled to his men, "Be ready! Fire as soon as you can get a target!"

CHAPTER 19

MARCH 28, PRE DAWN

WELL BEFORE DAWN, REX GAVE his men one last speech before they started marching towards Fort Brazos. "Two days, and we're there. Two days, and all the food you can eat and all the women you could want. It's likely—almost certain, in fact—that we will see battle with their men today or tomorrow. I don't believe they will wait for us at the village. Remember, they're plow boys, and you are warriors. When they attack, hit them hard and hit them fast. Kill them out here, and the village will be sitting there like a ripe peach, just waiting for you." He noted with satisfaction that the men's response sounded like they were primed, ready, and eager, seeing visions of the easy life in the village that lay just ahead of them.

Rex told Frank, "Move them out."

Within minutes, Rex's men were under fire. Rex moved up front to get a closer look, it appeared that there were somewhere between twenty and forty men firing on them, but firing ineffectively. Rex shouted out, "We have them completely outnumbered and they aren't shooting worth a shit, try to pick your targets as we advance, take advantage of cover as you move up. This is it, boys, now move up!"

Rex, the consummate survivor, allowed the men to get out front as he waited. When the men were past him and he started to follow, the men suddenly started yelling and running forward. *What the hell?* he thought. Then it dawned on him. They were chasing after what they thought was a retreating enemy, images of the open village in their heads.

Rex knew he couldn't bring the men back—the coming storm and their strung out running had ended any chance of stopping them before they fell prey to the ambush he knew had to be just ahead. Rex grabbed Frank's arm and said, "They're dead; forget them. Grab anyone you can, and we'll move around the ambush and head for the village. If we can get there first, we can control them with hostages."

Frank disappeared for several minutes. The storm was on them full force now, a twister tearing up the earth only a few hundred yards away. Rex took cover by lying down and covering the back of his head.

CHAPTER 20

MARCH 28, EARLY MORNING

L INDA'S TEAM HAD HELD THEIR position through the storm. They were cold, shivering, and bruised from the hail. The rain was almost gone and she could hear constant gunfire from the ambush. The sun was coming up and the clouds were thinning out, the light much better than before. She could once again see the battle area, but dimly. It looked like Adrian's plan was working. Firing was steady from the surrounding men, but declining from those surrounded. The village men appeared to be taking a horrific toll on the raiders. She began to feel the stirrings of elation, of victory, but quickly pushed them back down. Too soon to celebrate; anything could still happen. She moved up and down the line, reassuring the women and steadying them. The battle had been going on for over an hour, with half of it seemingly stopped by the storm. For now, all she could do was watch and wait...and hope.

Adrian waited for a target, he said to Bollinger, "I'm worried. This is going entirely too well, and too quickly."

Bollinger replied, "What do you mean?"

"I mean, we seem to be winning too quickly. Before

the storm hit, it looked like all hell was firing back at us, like every single raider was shooting. During the storm, we lost visual contact with them for nearly thirty minutes. Now it seems there are significantly less firing back. Are they running out of ammunition, holding their fire as they gather for a surge, or did we kill more than I thought originally? My gut tells me something isn't kosher."

"Damn, Adrian. We're kicking their ass in spite of being hit by a tornado, and you're going all pessimistic? What's the matter? They are a bunch of ragtag, starving raiders that just got hit by a major ambush, and you know it."

"Rex—that's what's the matter. Rex doesn't go down this easily. He should have concentrated his men on one spot and charged his men straight at it by now. He wouldn't just sit still and let his men be slowly picked off. Something's wrong. Either we didn't get Rex and all his men into the draw and he's still outside somewhere, or he got out in the middle of the storm."

"Or we got lucky and he's dead," Bollinger replied.

"Well, we can hope," Adrian replied and squeezed off another shot.

"Look! They're making a surge right at us!" Bollinger shouted.

Adrian began choosing target after target, firing almost continuously, as were the rest of his group. The raiders kept coming although they were being mowed down. The last ten men threw down their guns and raised their hands in surrender. They fell almost instantly as they were cut down by multiple rifles. Then there was only ear ringing silence, as all firing had stopped. Adrian watched and waited a full five minutes. The light fog from the storm's aftermath still drifted knee high in wisps. Adrian had a continuing sense of foreboding. *Too easy, too complete*, he thought.

MARCH 28, MID MORNING

Adrian rose from his position, stood surveying the scene. Muddy water was running swiftly down the draw from the rain, bodies were scattered throughout the draw. He carefully began moving forward, signaling for only three men to join him. Bollinger and two other men joined him, and they slowly worked their way down the draw, looking at bodies, checking every place that a still-living raider might be laying in ambush or hiding. There were raiders still alive, incapacitated by their wounds. A single bullet was fired into the head of those who were alive, and those whose wounds didn't look mortal. There was no mercy in these shootings, only finality.

Adrian waved his men down from their positions, gathered them together, and said, "Rex is not among the dead, and the dead don't total up to his full strength. There are at least twenty men missing, including Rex. The son of a bitch is still out there loose somewhere." Before he could say anything else, they heard gunfire and then four huge booms almost together coming from the women's position behind them. After the explosions, there was a scattering of shots, then silence again. Adrian raised his voice, "Stand. The women followed us out of the village, and that gunfire is coming from their position." Signaling to ten of the men with him, he said, "You men come with me; the rest come up behind us slowly in a wide line. We have to close in carefully, or the women may start firing at us."

Adrian told Bollinger, "Stretch the rest of them out and bring them on; look out for the raiders—they may still be between us and the women. We're going to move fast." Adrian then told his small team, "Follow me and don't get ahead of me!" He turned and began swiftly running toward the women.

He rapidly gained on his men, running faster than any of them could. As Adrian began to close in on the women, he saw bodies strewn on the ground in front of the group. The bodies were mangled and ripped apart. He slowed and waved his arms, wanting the women to see him clearly. As he got closer, Linda yelled out "Come on, we see you." Adrian picked up his pace and joined her. Without wasting time, he asked, "Did any escape?"

"A bunch of raiders came right at us that must have gotten around you. We hit them, mostly with Matt's cannons, but a handful of them disappeared into those trees." She pointed to a tree line in the distance.

"Casualties?"

"None—well, maybe some hearing loss from those cannons. Damn things are loud. No, they barely returned fire. Getting hit with those chains at close range with no warning rocked them back hard."

"Why did you leave the village?" Adrian asked.

"Remember when you told me I had to act autonomously? It was my decision, and I stand by it."

Adrian replied. "Turned out to be a good one. Could have been a disaster, but you did well."

Adrian's men arrived as he finished talking and heard what she said. Adrian said, "Linda, the rest of the men will be coming up soon. Send a runner to Bollinger and tell him where the raiders disappeared. Tell him to send his fastest men to cut them off in case they are heading towards the village. Tell those men to be damn careful who they shoot at, because we're going to have men spread out all over the place to try and locate Rex." Adrian quickly checked the bodies; he didn't think Rex's would be among them, and it wasn't." He counted sixteen bodies.

Adrian told his men, "We're going to head west into those trees and see if they're still there, the other men will be getting between them and the village. Come on, let's roll." He led the men at a slightly slower pace, since they had just sprinted half a mile across broken country and wouldn't be able to maintain his own pace. Adrian was cursing with almost every step, "Son of a bitch, son of a bitch, son of a bitch."

MARCH 28, LATE AFTERNOON

Adrian eventually sent his group out as runners to bring everyone back to the village. Rex and the men with him had disappeared; there was no indication where they went. Adrian waited while everyone trickled back into the village. Bollinger reported, "We lost six men, and fourteen were wounded. Of the wounded, three are critical and may not make it. We, plus the women, killed all but four of the raiders. For all intents and purposes the raiders are done. There's no sign yet of the snipers, but I've got men out searching for them. We've retrieved all of our fallen. They'll be prepared for burial tomorrow. All of the wounded are in the hospital being worked on. The raiders' bodies are where they fell, and we stripped them of weapons and ammo. Do we plan to do anything with their bodies?"

Adrian replied, "No, we leave them there. They can feed the buzzards; it's the best use they ever had."

"Adrian," Bollinger said with a sudden gravity, "Clif was killed. Took a bullet through his throat."

Adrian stood stock still, his falling face giving away his pain at the news. "Aw, fuck!" he suddenly shouted. *Goddamn that Rex to a burning fucking hell!* Adrian walked away from everyone, his fists clenched. He stopped when he was out of earshot. For a long five minutes, he stood with his back turned. His shoulders were hunched, moving up and down. It was obvious he was crying, and just as obvious that he didn't want to be disturbed. Finally, his shoulders eased as the crying ended. Wiping his eyes, Adrian turned around and came back to his men.

His face was as grim as Bollinger had ever seen it. His eyes were red and his cheeks were still wet. "Thanks for telling me. He was the best—the very best. We'll have a wake for him when this is over. We'll get drunker than shit and raise him up. But not now; now it's time to finish this. I'll kill that fucking Rex if it's the last thing I do."

Adrian raised his voice so that the gathering men could hear him. "We won a major battle today, but the war isn't over until Rex is dead. The problem is that he can hit and run at his place of choosing and when he wants to. Unless he has turned tail and run off—which I don't believe—he'll be a major problem for everyone. If we send scouts out, he'll pick them off. Even the best trained of us will be at a disadvantage because we'll have to move around to find him. Even if a scout spots him, he can't attack and win. Rex and his men will be too good for one man to take on. If a scout returns with information on where Rex is, he won't be there when we go out in strength.

"Spread the word to everyone that we have a critical sniper situation. Rex is likely to come close, shoot one or two people, and then disappear, only to return sometime later to repeat. He can keep that up forever, as I well know. Until he gets what he wants, he'll just keep on killing. He'll kill women and children as quickly as men. In fact, he may target women and children specifically—that's a more effective terror tactic than killing men.

"I have a strong feeling that his true target in this whole expedition of his has been me all along. The sick bastard couldn't care less about the village; he just used that to manipulate his men to draw me back home. This is a personal vendetta that's eating up his twisted mind. As long as I am here the villagers will never be safe. I have to leave, draw him away, and deal with him on my own. He wants personal, well, he's going to get a lot more personal than he really wants. I'll leave by morning, but we need to figure out some way to let him know I'm gone."

Matt, Perry, and Tim were still near the ambush zone. They knew the battle was over, had closed in at the last minute and joined in the ambush. But Roman was still unaccounted for. Without a word to each other, they took off looking for him. They walked toward where they though he might have been, back behind the lines. They were afraid they were looking for his body, but no one would say so. Matt, an avid hunter, a good tracker, but the storm had wiped out any possibility of finding tracks. They moved spread out in as wide a line as they could and maintain visual contact. They had been walking for two hours when they heard three gunshots deliberately spaced out two seconds apart. It was a classic signal for help.

Tim said, "That has to be Roman. Told you he was lost!"

The three men quickly headed for where the sound had come from. The shots had been fairly close. Within half an hour, they heard three more shots, much closer this time. They tried to hurry, but they were now working their way directly through the path of the tornado and it was strewn with broken trees, making them detour or climb over them often. Well before dark they found him. He was pinned under a tree, laying on his stomach, and looked like he had been run through a meat grinder. He was covered with blood from what looked like a dozen cuts and scrapes. He had a large splinter sticking out of his shoulder, but he was alive and clearly alert.

Roman said in a hoarse voice, "Did we win? What the hell took y'all so long to get here? I thought I was going to have to gnaw this damn tree off of me."

Perry said, "We won; not sure if they got Rex or not, though. Grit your teeth—I'm going to pull this splinter out." Perry pulled it out and Roman grunted at the sharp pain.

"Damn good thing we won, or I'd be sorely pissed." Roman said.

Tim asked, "Any broken bones or bad cuts?"

"Naw, I think I'm okay, just a little skint up and stuck in the mud under this damn tree. It just pushed me down into the mud. Lucky thing I was laying in this depression to begin with. Dig me out, will you?"

While the men dug mud from under and around Roman, Matt asked him, "How the hell did you get under a tree, you old fart? What were you doing way back here, anyway—you get lost again?"

Roman turned his head and gave Tim the stink eye. "You been telling them about me getting lost in San Angelo?"

"Yep, told them you got lost three times in three days," Tim said with a wicked grin. "But I didn't tell them about you getting lost on the golf course in Abilene."

"Well, you just did, you fucking retard," Roman replied with a growl.

Tim laughed; Roman was definitely okay.

Roman explained what had happened as he was being eased out from under the tree by six not too gentle hands. "I snuck through their lines yesterday and started hitting them from behind, thought it would give them even more to think about. Couldn't get back across their lines, so I stayed back of them and kept hitting them. Then, just at dark, I saw them setting up a camouflaged wall tent, and figured it would be Rex's since it was way bigger than anyone else's. But it was too dark to do anything, so I sat there waiting for daylight. Thought I might get a chance to pick him off in the morning. Because of the damn storm it never did get light enough, but for a moment, I thought I spotted him during a series of lightning flashes. Big, tall blond-headed guy walking around like he owned the world. Tried to get a shot, but it started raining real hard, so I hunkered down to wait some more, hoping for a shot.

"Did you fellas see that tornado? I didn't see it coming where I was, just all of a sudden I could hear it, and then the damn thing seemed to be right on top of me. I laid as flat as I could in the lowest spot I could find, even though it was full of water. Whoo-whee, but the wind was blowing hard, hail was hitting me, trees were flying by, grass was being sucked up into the air roots and all. Thought the wind was going to rip my clothes off. Never seen anything like it. Scared the crap out of me; I thought I was a goner for sure. Then this damn tree fell across me and got me stuck, it might have saved my life, keeping me from being sucked up into the air. Tried, but couldn't reach around to dig myself out, so finally I started shooting, hoping we'd won and someone would hear me. Figured if the bad guys showed up and shot me, it would be better than starving to death.

"Boys, thank you very much for finding me. When we get home, drinks are on me. And lots of them."

As he watched Roman rubbing his lower back and limping toward home, Matt said, "You better let one of us lead the way so you don't get lost again, don't you think?"

Roman replied, "Screw you, Matt. Just remember who makes the whisky."

MARCH 29, PRE DAWN

Adrian spent the rest of the day arguing with everyone about going after Rex alone. Every single man—and Linda, too—wanted to go with him. He had to make the same case over and over. "Look," Adrian said to Linda, "Rex has a disadvantage: he has two or three men with him. That makes it extremely difficult to move quickly. He has to stop to explain everything to those men, and hope they understand. He has to move swiftly and quietly, but with four men, there are four times as many mistakes that will be made. I wouldn't be surprised if he kills them. They're a burden now. I don't want that disadvantage. I don't want to have to constantly explain the next move or to have to watch out for anyone else's life. What I have to do is best done alone."

Linda replied, "I see what you mean, but it just doesn't sit right with me knowing that you are going to be out there alone against Rex and his men while we sit here and wait. Adrian, there's something else, too. I—" She stuttered to a stop. "I...want you to be very careful," she finally said, wanting to say more but unable get the words out.

Adrian looked at her for a long time and then said, "I'll do my best. I'm going to leave before daylight, move around the area and choose where I would attack from if I were doing what I think Rex is going to do. I have signs I'll post at those locations. When I get back, there are some things I want to say to you."

Linda felt hope mixed with dread, and asked, "What signs? What for?" She thought she knew what Adrian wanted to talk to her about, but she was afraid she might be wrong. She wouldn't push, didn't want to face hearing what she was afraid she might hear.

"I have to let Rex know I am not in the village in order to draw him away. I made signs with poster board that say, 'Rex, I'm out here looking for you, Adrian.' I know it's kind of lame, but it's the best I could think of, and I believe it will work. If he thinks I'm out there looking for him, I don't think he'll expose himself by shooting at villagers, because I could find him quickly if he did. But I could be wrong, so everyone In the village will have to be extra careful all the same, at least until I come back. No one should go out hunting, until this is over; they could get killed."

Lind asked, "So what's your plan when you get out there? How long will it take?"

"I don't know how long it will take. Days, weeks—maybe even a month."

Adrian then explained his plan to Linda. When he was done, she nodded her head and said, "It could work, Adrian, it could work. Just be as careful as you can and come back safe." Without thinking about it, she gave him a quick hug and a quicker kiss on the lips, then turned and fled, leaving Adrian bemused.

CHAPTER 21

MARCH 30, MID DAY

B Y NOON, ADRIAN HAD PLACED three of the posters. He had covered a circle halfway around Fort Brazos. The other three posters would cover the other half of the circle. That would be enough, Adrian believed. He had been moving slowly and cautiously, looking for any sign of Rex as he went. Adrian knew the area thoroughly; he already knew the spots that would most likely attract Rex. Under normal circumstances he could have placed all six posters in only a couple of hours. These weren't normal circumstances, though. He had a cold-blooded, highly trained, highly skilled, and experienced killer with a psychotic obsession of hunting for him, and while Adrian wanted to be found, he wanted to be found on his own terms. He wanted control of the situation when they fought.

By dark, he had the six posters placed. Now it was time to start on the second phase. Adrian walked back to the battlefield where the bodies were lying. Using a flashlight, he chose a dead raider that was nearly his size and had the same color hair. It was a gruesome task he had in mind, but he would carry it through.

Heaving the already deteriorating body across his shoulders, he carried it the several miles to his chosen spot. It took him until nearly midnight to reach the area he wanted. He tossed the body on the ground, and in the dark, he stripped the man's clothes off. Adrian had left several items in that spot earlier in the day; among them were the clothes that Adrian had worn during the battle. It was a struggle dressing the body in his clothes It was disgusting work, but it had to be done.

Adrian pushed up a pile of leaves a few yards from the body and lay down exhausted; it had been a long day. He had a restless night with strange dreams of being in the future, a place where tiny robots were injected into his blood stream. These robots provided access to knowledge he had never been exposed to. When he awoke, the dream stayed with him for most of the day, the images slowly fading.

At first light, Adrian began his preparations. He placed the body facedown next to a fallen log. With his knife, he ripped the body open with long slashes, imitating the cuts that a wild boar would have made. Then he opened a gallon jar of pig blood, which was already coagulating, and splashed and spread the blood on the "wounds" he had made, as well as on the log. Using a broken tree branch, he tore up the ground around the body as though there had been a big fight. He took his battle rifle, emptied the ammo, and placed the rounds in his pocket, reinserted the magazine, and then tossed the rifle next to the body. Standing back, he viewed his work. From a few yards away, it looked exactly as he wanted it to: as though Adrian had been attacked by a wild boar and lost the fight.

Adrian made a blood trail leading away from the body, imitating a wounded hog leaving the area. The blood trail gradually disappeared a hundred yards away.

Adrian had chosen this spot carefully. A place where the body would be visible from the higher ground around it.

MARCH 31, MID DAY

Adrian wanted Rex to spot the body and assume it was Adrian. He knew that Rex wouldn't be deceived when he came close to investigate, but by then, Adrian would have him in his sights. He also knew that if Rex did spot the body from a distance, he would have to move closer to investigate. Adrian had chosen the terrain well. Rex could approach from any direction, and would move in extremely cautiously. Rex was far from a fool and would suspect a trap, but he would have to check it out.

Adrian built and set three booby-traps, one at each of the most likely approaches that he thought Rex might take. Two of them were punji pits. If Rex stepped into one of them, it wouldn't kill him, but it would slow him down quite a bit, an advantage Adrian would like to have. Eventually, the poisoned sharpened stakes would kill Rex if he didn't get medical treatment. Adrian didn't have much hope for these working, but they might.

The third trap was more complex. He'd made it with one of Matt's hog guns loaded with double ought buck shot. The double-barreled gun was secured in a horizontal position and tied down then hidden with brush artfully arranged. A trip line of monofilament fishing line was placed under tension across the path, strung out an inch above the ground and then lightly covered with leaves. If Rex took that path and either stepped on the trip line or snagged it with his foot, the trip line would pull the trigger, unleashing a barrel of buck shot down the trail. The traps also served another purpose: they were located behind Adrian's line of sight, and if one of them worked, it would act as a signal so Adrian could then leap to the attack.

By midday, Adrian had taken up his hiding position. He had chosen a simple but daring plan. He scooped out a spot in the ground that he could lay down flat in, hiding the dirt as he worked. Adrian placed a self-inflating sleeping pad in the depression. He lay down on his belly with his rifle in position, then, using his hands and a tree branch, he covered his body with leaves that he had brought in and piled up next to his shallow trench. Adrian covered his head last, carefully placing leaves over and around his face, leaving spaces to look through. From even a half dozen steps away, he was invisible under the leaves. He had a field of fire that covered the decoy body and the surrounding fifty yards. It would be an easy shot; only seventy-five yards away, and the rifle would only have to move a few inches to cover any part of the trap radius.

MARCH 31, EVENING

Once in place, Adrian was committed to lying still for however long it took. He was well aware that he might lie there for several days and would become extremely uncomfortable. He was also aware that if he had to move suddenly, his body would be stiff and slow. The self-inflating sleeping pad under him would insulate him from the ground, helping to maintain his body temperature. The thick pile of leaves above him would not only conceal him, but also help keep him a little warmer than lying directly exposed to the cold night and morning air. He had placed a canteen of water and a drinking tube of flexible plastic tubing ran from it into his mouth. He would not be eating for the duration, but he would need to stay hydrated. He would just have to urinate in place; messy, but necessary under the circumstances. . From now until he either trapped Rex or gave up waiting, it was all about mental discipline. Not moving, not scratching, just lying completely still—it was unnatural for a human, and was difficult to do for even an hour; doing so for days would be excruciating.

Time passed slowly. Mosquitoes found his face through the leaves and bit him almost continuously. It took all of his willpower to let them feast undisturbed. Adrian marked the passing of time during the day by tracking the movement of shadows. He slept only at night, and even then only in brief snatches. He could see a portion of the sky through a gap in the trees, and watched as stars moved in and then out of the gap. He meditated often, slowing his breathing. In between meditations, starting from his toes and moving up to his face, he slowly tensed one muscle group at a time and held the tension for as long as he could, then moved on to the next muscle group. To occupy his mind, he timed how long he could maintain tension in each muscle group by silently counting off the seconds. This exercise kept his blood from pooling in his extremities without him making overt movements.

He hoped it would keep him from being too stiff when the time came to move.

Adrian observed the wildlife. A possum found the body and feasted on it for an hour before wandering off. Twice he saw deer browsing. He watched squirrels by the dozen and birds by the hundreds move around the area. He listened carefully for a sudden silence of birds or a squirrel fussing or a deer snorting or stamping— signs of something or someone coming. Adrian focused his attention on sounds by mentally charting out a full circle and dividing it into quarters. Every five minutes or so, he would focus on the next quarter in the circle and pay attention to just that one section. It didn't take him long to pattern out the normal sounds. He knew where several squirrels called home, where different birds had staked out their territories. He became familiar with the hunting ranges of the owls at night. Adrian absorbed all this conscientiously because his natural radar system would alert him to the presence of something or someone that didn't belong.

Of all the challenges he faced, staying mentally alert was the hardest. It was too easy to drift off into irrelevant thought, or to focus on the discomforts of being completely still. The meditation, muscle tension exercises, shifting his focus on listening to specific quadrants, and the occasional small sip of water were the only antidotes to mental distraction. They worked to a degree, but he still had to periodically bring his mind back to a focus after it had drifted off.

Frequently, his thoughts drifted to Linda and that parting hug and kiss. The more he thought about it, the more he became convinced that the feelings he was having for her were returned. It was natural, he supposed. Both of them had lost a loved one; both of them were in the physical prime of their lives. Being pushed together during a time of extreme stress and relying on each other for survival would naturally create a bond. She was an attractive woman, and not just physically; she was full of surprises. He liked her tough mental attitude, her ability to face her fears and keep moving forward. He loved the way she spoke honestly in line with her own integrity. She was, he knew, a prime candidate for a life-mate, especially so in this dangerous post-grid world. With plenty of time to think about her and the situation they were in, he became convinced that her parting kiss had been her way of saying how she felt about him, a sign that only a fool could ignore. He thought, *well, when I get back, I'll look into that, but right now, I have to concentrate!*

APRIL 1, LATE MORNING

By day two of his vigil, the decoy body had begun to swell up and smell. Adrian would catch strong whiffs of it whenever the breeze blew in his direction. Fortunately, it mostly blew away from him. A few times, the wind blew with enough strength to scatter the leaves around on the ground. Any traces of his manipulating the leaves over him had been erased by those winds. No one would be able see any difference between where he lay now and the forest floor. It had sprinkled rain twice, light rains that penetrated the leaves and soaked his clothes. He was alternately hot and cold, depending on the shadow patterns as they moved during the day. The mosquitos were still working his face over, and he knew that it would be a nasty mess, but it would heal. He couldn't wait to scratch at least three thousand places on his body, and would as soon as he could.

Adrian could occasionally hear the hum of flies that swarmed over the body. A small hog had found the body by following the stench, and had fed on it before wandering off again. *All to the good,* he thought. It made the body harder to identify as not his, and would help it look as natural as it should have.

Another long night passed in short bursts of deep sleep. The dream came back each night, but it was less intense each time. Visions of future humans that acted queerly flitted through his sleep. It was an odd sort of dream that Adrian thought about a lot, but could not decipher any meaning from.

It was on the third day that something slowly crept into his awareness as he lay aching and itching. He had become intimately attuned to the sounds around him, and slowly, he became aware of a small silence in the far background as birds quieted. He focused, listening, and noted that there was a circle of silence slowly moving toward him. It was still a long way off, but there was definitely something there. It could be a pack of hogs, or coyotes, a bobcat, or a hunter. Or Rex. Adrian strained to listen. He heard a squirrel begin fussing in the silent zone. Something was definitely moving there, something the native wildlife didn't like.

CHAPTER 22

MARCH 28, EARLY MORNING

FRANK HAD QUICKLY GATHERED NINETEEN men, and Rex moved out and around the ambush during the storm. Circling around it, he had headed toward the village only to suddenly be fired on by some kind of ordnance from well behind the ambush lines. *Damn that Adrian*, he thought. The bastard had left a backup group and they had spotted him and his men. Sixteen of his men were brutally mowed down. He and the other three took off running before they could be fired on again.

Once past the secondary skirmish line, Rex stopped and took stock. He knew pursuit would only be minutes behind. "Frank, take these three men and head out in any direction away from the village. You men are on your own now. I suggest you get as far away from here as you can, and if you're smart, you'll all go in different directions. If I see any of you again, I'll kill you. Stay away from the village; I don't want any interference. Now get going!"

Without a backward glance, Rex headed east as fast as he could. When he had placed enough distance between him and any pursuers, he found a pile of downed trees and crawled inside them to rest. *I've got Adrian where I want him. He won't stay in the village knowing I'm out here. It's just a matter of time before I locate and capture him, and then the fun begins.* Rex's hand unconsciously stroked his "Adrian Bag" while he hid. He remained there a full twenty-four hours, resting up, thinking and planning.

When he was ready to move, he crawled out of the blow down and carefully looked around. Opening his bag, he removed the crossbow and began assembling it. "Adrian is in for a big surprise, and not a happy one," he said out loud. Then he began laughing.

CHAPTER 23

APRIL 2, EARLY AFTERNOON

WHATEVER WAS MOVING TOWARD HIM was moving slowly. Adrian listened and waited. It could be Rex. It was moving slower than he would expect a hog or coyote to move. It was moving with such slowness that it was clear that it was trying to be stealthy. Sweat ran down his mosquito bite-ravaged face, setting up a fierce itching sensation. He carefully drew in a full mouthful of water and slowly swallowed it, then another one. Hunger had initially bothered him, but had receded to a dull sensation. He flexed and released all the muscle groups over and over. He wanted as much blood flow as possible, but he was careful to not move even a tiny bit otherwise.

The silent area was at the edge of his vision when he saw Rex—or part of Rex. He was moving with extreme care and slowness. When Rex reached the point where he could see the decoy body, he stopped. Rex didn't move for over an hour, only turning his head slowly to scan around him. Twice, he looked directly to where Adrian lay, but displayed no sign of alarm or interest in the area. He was not in a spot where Adrian could move to shoot him without giving himself away too soon. Adrian was no longer aware of the itching or thirst or anything else. He was completely focused on Rex, and Rex was alone.

Rex stayed still for so long that the birds and squirrels had lost interest and had gone back to their normal movements and sounds. Rex began to move again, this time even more slowly than before. As he gradually came into full view, Adrian was surprised to see that Rex was carrying a crossbow, his rifle slung over his shoulder. Ever so slowly, Rex moved to a new position where he could see the body more clearly, but still he did not move into Adrian's target area. He was within range, but wasn't positioned at a good angle.

Rex stopped and pulled out a pair of binoculars and studied the body for a solid fifteen minutes without moving. Then he began to move back again, to Adrian's right and further away. Rex disappeared. Adrian didn't know if he had figured out it wasn't his body or not. With the leaves strewn across it, the damage done by the hog, and the flesh swelling up, Adrian knew it would be damned hard for Rex to be certain. He hoped he wouldn't leave the area without giving Adrian a shot.

Adrian closed his eyes and concentrated on listening again. He wondered why Rex would use a crossbow. It didn't have the range of a rifle, and once the shooting started, noise would no longer matter. Rex would only get one shot with it, then he would either have to take the time to reload, or take off back into the woods and get his rifle off his back and into position. It didn't make sense. Giving up trying to decipher Rex's thinking, Adrian listened and waited. *Patience*, he kept thinking, *I'll probably only get one clear shot. Patience, patience; make that one shot count.*

APRIL 2, MID AFTERNOON

Rex was moving so slowly that it was difficult to tell where he was. There was a sudden flutter of wings, and the sounds of a squirrel running through the leaves and scurrying up a tree trunk gave Adrian a fairly precise idea of where Rex was. Adrian listened, catching an occasional clue. Rex was getting closer to Adrian, coming up behind him. Knowing the terrain, Adrian guessed where Rex was moving to for a different view of the body. Rex smelled a trap, no doubt of that. Adrian had known he would, but then again, it was just barely possible enough that it was Adrian's body down there that Rex would have to take the time to thoroughly check it out—he couldn't afford not to. Even if Rex moved away, Adrian would find him. He would slowly rise up from his position and become the hunter, and Rex the hunted. It would end this day, one way or another. Adrian was satisfied his trap had performed its function, even if Rex left the area without giving Adrian a shot.

Rex was moving closer again, toward the body. He was definitely angling for a better look. Adrian waited, and waited, and still had to wait. Slowly, parts of Rex became visible again to Adrian's extreme right field of view. There was a break in the brush that Rex was headed for. It would be a spot where Adrian could take a shot, but he would have to rise up while twisting to get into alignment first. If Rex reached that spot and began backing away again, Adrian knew he would have take his best shot. He would have to move extremely fast, risking that his muscles weren't too tight. He would have less than a second to move and fire.

Extremely slowly, Rex moved to the notch in the brush. He was extraordinarily cautious, slowly rotating his head from side to side, looking at everything with focus. He was clearly suspicious of a trap, but wasn't sure of it. He reached the spot. Taking his binoculars out again in super slow motion, he studied the body. Adrian noticed a very slight tensing of Rex's body. He knew this meant he had decided it wasn't Adrian down there. If he had thought it was Adrian, he wouldn't have tensed that little bit. Rex now knew it was a trap, and began moving back again. He was forty yards away. Adrian tensed all his muscles at the same time, relaxed them, and then rose up as quickly as he could to his knees while twisting his torso to bring the rifle to bear. His body screamed in protest, his muscles nearly locking up completely. Rex immediately saw him and twisted toward him, bringing up the crossbow at the same time Adrian brought up the rifle. They both fired at the same time.

Adrian's muscles spasamed as he fired, his aim thrown off enough that he barely hit Rex's shoulder, not a disabling wound. Rex's snap shot with the crossbow was on target, hitting Adrian to the left of the center of his chest, the missile burying into Adrian.

Rex immediately disappeared back into the brush before Adrian could shoot again. Adrian looked down at his chest, expecting to see an arrow sticking out of it. He stared in disbelief for a full two seconds before it registered that he was looking at a serum dart—the type used to tranquilize large animals. He had no idea what had just been injected into him, whether it was poison or a tranquilizer. He realized he might only have seconds left to live and jerked out the dart, jumping to his feet and running as fast as he could toward the shotgun booby trap he had set earlier. His muscles were cramping and screaming after so long without motion. As he ran, he felt his legs shutting down. He could no longer feel his feet, and his legs were wildly out of control. Adrian staggered and fell next to the trip line, falling on his back. His last hope was that Rex would trip the line and get hit by the buckshot when he came to investigate Adrian's condition. Rex had the upper hand now; he could shoot him from a distance or walk up close and shoot him from close range. Adrian's hoped the paralysis would be temporary, and that Rex would come closer to gloat and in the process trip the wire. It wasn't much of a hope. Even if Rex tripped the wire, the odds of him being in line with the shotgun and getting hit were at best 50/50.

He was completely paralyzed now; he couldn't even blink. He lay staring up at the sky, conscious and aware of his surroundings. He lay there for what seemed like hours but was, in fact, only minutes. He was still breathing, but shallowly. He heard Rex walking toward him, not trying to conceal the sound of his footsteps in the dry leaves. Then Rex's face loomed over him, looking down at him with the cruelest rictus of a smile that Adrian had ever seen. Rex was jubilant in his victory. He looked as if he had just received the absolute greatest gift that could ever have come his way. His eyes were malignant, evil.

Rex said, "You can't possibly imagine how much I have dreamed of this moment. How often I have pictured it. How absolutely driven I have been to have you like this. I have plans for you, Adrian, really big plans. Guess what? I'm not going to kill you...

but when I'm finished with you, you'll pray for death every second of every day that you live, and I think you're going to live for a long, long time, thanks to your hospital. How's that for irony? And guess what else? You won't be able to kill yourself, no matter how badly you're going to want to. Oh, this is perfect, just fucking wonderfully perfect!"

"I've dreamed of this, planned for this, and the plan is brilliant—absolutely brilliant. At first, I intended to amputate your arms and legs and then sew them up. But I was afraid that that amount of trauma would kill you, or that you would get an infection and die. So I worked it out to do the same thing in another way. I brought these plumber's hose clamps, see?" Rex held a clamp over Adrian's face. Adrian saw a metal strap with little slots cut in it and a screw mechanism to tighten it, like on a car's radiator hose, only larger. "I'm going to put these on your arms and legs, way up high on each one, then tighten the hell out of them. It will cut off the blood to your limbs, and by the time you're found, they'll have to be amputated. The amputation will be done by your doctor at your hospital to save your life. Oh, he'll hate to do it, but he will do it. You know how doctors are—got to save that life, right?

"The rest is quick and simple: I'll cut out your tongue and cauterize it with a hot knife to stop the bleeding. You'll enjoy that, won't you? Then a screwdriver, driven into each ear to burst the eardrums so you won't be able to hear. Oh, I'll heat it up until it's red-hot first so there won't be any bacteria to infect you—beautiful, eh? The screwdriver that tightens the clamp serves three purposes. Last but most certainly not least, I push the red-hot screwdriver slowly into your eyes, blinding you in a most exquisite way.

"You see what will be left? No arms, no legs, can't talk, can't hear, and can't see—oh, and bonus! You won't be able to taste the baby food they feed you. You'll be able to feel sensations in your body, and think, oh you'll think a lot. You'll have Itches you can't scratch, and pains that you can't do anything about except endure. Your mind will be locked into a dark place with no input except pain. You'll go insane, and best of all, you'll stay insane and won't be able to do a damn thing about it except hate me, hate knowing that I am still alive and whole. You'll spend the rest of your life in impotent rage and hate. I'll enjoy that; I'll think about it all the time. For as long as you live, I will be laughing my ass off at you. But wait, there's more! As they said on TV. When I know you're dead, I'm going to come back and kill your family, one at a vicious time.

"You can ponder on that and try to stay alive as long as possible, hoping I die before you do." Rex started laughing, a wild, cacophonous laughter. Then suddenly, he stopped laughing and just leered at Adrian.

Adrian watched Rex's insane face, listened to his insane plan, and knew Rex would do exactly what he said. He knew Rex was right: trapped inside his brain like that, he would go insane and suffer agonies he could never imagine in his worst nightmares. Adrian couldn't close his eyes to stop looking up into that leering face above him. He realized that once Rex began putting the clamp on his right arm, he was done for, there would be nothing left he could do. There was only one thing he could try to do, a once normally inconsequential movement, and the odds were so stacked against him that it was a forlorn hope at best. But since it was the one and only thing that he could try to do, he would put everything he had into doing it.

Rex hadn't tripped the tripwire. He apparently hadn't seen it, either. Rex was squatted down more or less in line with the shotgun. If he would only move his arm two inches, he'd release the trip wire. Two tiny inches. If Rex picked that arm up to put on the clamp, it would be impossible to do it. It had to be now, while he was in full gloating mode, before he began to actually put the clamp on. Rex sounded like he would go on talking for a long time, but then again, Rex was aware of how long the paralysis would last, and Adrian wasn't. Adrian began by mentally closing his eyes. He couldn't physically close his eyes, but he could pretend they were closed and try to quit seeing that hate filled face. He didn't need that distraction. He also turned Rex's words into a buzzing noise—much less irritating. Then he began focusing his full consciousness on one thing and one thing only: moving that right arm onto the trip wire. A small movement under normal circumstances. A herculean task now.

Adrian couldn't feel his body. If he moved his arm, he wouldn't know it. He couldn't turn his head to see it. If his arm started to move, he wouldn't be aware of it. He knew that any doctor would have told him it was physically impossible. As Adrian considered all this in the span of a few seconds, he considered that the serum must be at least three years old and might have weakened over time. Although Rex couldn't tell it, Adrian was no longer paying him any attention. Rex might as well not have been there.

Adrian began concentrating on his right elbow. He intensely imagined bending that elbow up and to his right, and then letting the arm fall. Such a small thing. He focused, really focused every bit of his mind on that small action. He visualized it, saw it in his mind's eye as happening, put every fiber of his being into making it happen. He made himself believe, really truly believe that his arm was up and over the tripwire, made himself believe it with every shred of his being, and then he visualized letting go, letting the arm drop.

As he did, he heard a rustle of leaves immediately to his right, then a huge booming sound. Rex made a startled noise. Then there was silence for a second, and Rex said, "Damn you to hell! Damn—" followed by gurgling sounds. Adrian couldn't see Rex; he was out of his cone of vision. He heard what sounded like a body falling, then a short period of thrashing. Then silence. Complete, blessed silence.

Adrian lay immobile, paralyzed and numb. He watched leaves fall, clouds move across the sky, the light disappear as the sun set. After a while, he could see stars moving across the sky through the tree limbs. He didn't know if he would ever move again, but he was content with whatever fate brought him now. Even if a wild hog found him and ate him alive, it would be better than what Rex had planned and almost succeeded at.

CHAPTER 24

APRIL 3, MID MORNING

URING THE NIGHT, THE EFFECTS of the chemical had slowly begun to wear off. Adrian hadn't realized it was diminishing. He slept, unaware that his eyes had closed. He had vivid dreams of a strange future. It was the last time he would dream of it. In the morning, he was awakened by a fierce itching on his face. His hand came up and began scratching before he was even awake enough to realize he was able to move. When he did, he smiled, and slowly and painfully rolled over. He looked right into Rex's face. The body was stiff now with rigor mortis. It lay on its side, facing Adrian, a look of total rage frozen on its dead face. Rex's eyes were open, but glazed over and murky. It was an ugly sight, but Adrian was delighted to see it. Rex's chest was a bloody mess from the buckshot. Adrian said a silent and fervent prayer of thanks.

He was dehydrated and weak with hunger. The drug that Rex had shot into his body had largely dissipated, but was still lingering. He had a raging headache. He tried to stand, but was too wobbly to walk. He crawled slowly on his hands and knees to where he had stashed his pack, which contained food and water. When he finally reached it, he was too weak and exhausted to do more than gulp several large swallows of water. He rested for nearly an hour, and then dug into the pack and pulled out one of the ration bars. He chewed slowly, taking frequent sips of water. He lay there for most of the day, slowly eating and drinking. When darkness came, he worked his way back into his trench and covered himself with leaves, and then he fell into a deep sleep.

Birds singing woke him late the next morning. He slowly stood and found he could walk a little. He removed everything from his pack but two ration bars and the water, and began carefully walking home. Adrian found a piece of limb strong enough to be used as a walking stick, and he used it as he went. He stopped to rest frequently, eating and drinking when he did. His strength was coming back, the headache was almost gone, and he was feeling better by the hour. He didn't make it home, however, before darkness overtook him. Adrian spent another night sleeping under the stars.

APRIL 5, MID MORNING

As Adrian approached the outskirts of Fort Brazos, Linda spotted him from her guard position. She exclaimed "Adrian! Thank God you're alive!" She rushed to him and gave him a terrific hug. She wrinkled her nose at the smell of stale urine and sour body odor, but didn't let go.

Adrian replied, "I am, but it was a close thing for a while."

Linda noticed his weakened state and mosquito bite-swollen face and quickly put his arm over her shoulders to help support him. She asked, "Did you get Rex?"

Adrian said, "More or less. He's dead, anyway. No more problems from him. Everything all right back home?"

"Yes, everything is fine. Now that you're back, everything is fine. I was...we were all scared you wouldn't come back." Linda looked into Adrian's eyes. Something in them gave her the courage to say, "I...I don't know what I would have done...I...I don't think I could have..." She buried her face in his chest for a moment, regaining control. "I know you probably think I'm silly, but...I think I have fallen in love with you." She kept her face against his chest, waiting for his reply.

In a soft voice that filled her with a trembling hope, a voice she felt rumbling in his chest as much as she heard it said, "I think I'm falling in love with you, too, Linda. It's just...it seems too soon to be decent. Alice has only been gone a little over a year. But the world is different now. We have to lead with our hearts in this world. We don't have the time we used to have. Either of us could be gone tomorrow. There're so many dangers now. But part of me can't let go of Alice, not yet."

Linda replied, "I feel the same way. My husband hasn't been gone that long, either. My feelings for you are not a betrayal of him, and your feelings for me aren't a betrayal of Alice, either. In a way, there are four of us to consider: ourselves and our ghosts. I believe that they loved us and would approve of us finding happiness again. Wouldn't they?" she asked.

"I think they would. If the shoe were on the other foot, I would want Alice to be happy. She was too young and full of life to grieve forever. I think I love you, Linda. But I'm not ready yet, and I can't take you with me where I'm going. You have a son to protect, and taking him with us wouldn't be protecting him. It's dangerous out there—hell, it's dangerous at Fort Brazos—but it's far too dangerous out there. Can you understand that?"

Linda replied, "No, I can't. Where are you going? Why can't you stay here?"

"Corpus Christi. I'm not ready to stay here. I have things I still have to do. If I don't do them, I'll...I'll be restless, unhappy. I'll regret not doing them every single day; every morning will have a bitter taste to it. It would come between us, and I don't want that. I will come back if you think you want me to, and can wait. You don't want me the way I would be if I didn't go. I need more time to say goodbye to Alice, too."

"I'll hate every day I have to wait. I'll wonder every day if you'll come back, and when. I can't imagine ever loving anyone else, Adrian, but I never thought I would love again before I met you. I'll try to wait, but I can't promise that I'll be here when you come back. If I fall in love with someone else—and I'm not saying I hope to, just that it apparently it could happen—then I'll have to move on with my life, Adrian."

Adrian replied, "One of the things I like best about you is that you're honest. You are brave and you are honest. I'd take you with me, but not your son—I couldn't risk his life. If something happened to him, you'd hate me for it. If you went, it would have to be because you made the decision. He wouldn't have that choice.

"I'm going to check out the rumors we've been hearing about the Navy using nuclear powered ships to set up a viable city in Corpus Christi. I have to see this with my own eyes, see if there is any way they can help the rest of us. Then I want to go down to the valley and come back up by way of San Antonio. Get a feel for how many villages and tribes there are, how they're surviving. See what I can learn that will be useful for us. See how Texas is doing. Then I'll come back home. I'm guessing a year, year and a half. It's a long time to wait, I know, and I have no right to ask it of you, so I won't ask it. If you're still here when I get back, we'll see how we feel then."

They arrived at the outskirts of Fort Brazos and were spotted by villagers. A cheer went up when they saw that Adrian was back. A small crowd quickly gathered. Adrian stopped. Still partially supported by Linda, he announced, "Rex is dead. The threat is over. There will be others, I imagine, but this one is gone." The cheering drew more people, and soon it seemed that the entire village was crowded around the couple.

Linda said, "Adrian is hurt and needs medical attention. Please, let's get him to the hospital." Within seconds, two of the larger men had picked Adrian up carefully and were carrying him to the hospital over his loud protests. When they arrived, Jennifer was waiting, having been forewarned. Adrian explained about the paralysis drug and the dehydration. The doctor quickly checked him over, put a salve on his face, and pronounced him fit enough for home bedrest for a few days until his strength returned. She said, "Sarah can give you the kind of treatment you need better than I can. The paralysis drug will have some lingering effects, but those will dissipate with time."

Despite his continuing protests, the two men carried Adrian to Roman's house with Linda walking beside them. The village had formed a line on either side of him, as though he were the center of a parade, cheering as he was carried by. Roman and Sarah were waiting at the house with big grins. The men deposited Adrian on the sofa and made mock bowing motions as they backed their way out of the room, smiling as they went. Linda, Bollinger, John, Isaac, Perry, Matt, and Tim all crowded around him, smiling and giving one another high fives as Adrian sat on the couch in embarrassment.

After a few minutes of this, Roman took control and said, "Look, folks, we all want to hear the story, but right now it looks like he needs rest more than anything. Let's all meet here again tomorrow at lunchtime, and if he is feeling up to it, he can tell the story then. Okay?"

They all took the hint and left, except for Linda. She sat next to Adrian, holding his hand. Sarah gave Linda a knowing look and said, "Linda, why don't you bring your son and that wolf pup over and spend the night? I could use some help, especially with all those men coming back for lunch tomorrow. My guess is they'll be here at breakfast instead of lunch."

Linda replied, "Be right back, Sarah." She took off almost running and was back quickly, Scott and Bear in tow. Bear sniffed Adrian over carefully and then curled up on his lap.

Sarah smiled and said, "You've got some explaining to do, young lady!" They went into the kitchen, made tea, and sat at the table talking until late that night. Roman was run out of the kitchen the one time he tried to come in to listen. "This is girl talk, old man. You just go on to bed," Sarah scolded him. Roman, pretending to have hurt feelings, turned and left.

APRIL 6, DAWN

Adrian awoke with the sun the next morning. Smelling bacon frying brought him out of a deep sleep, his stomach growling. He was famished. He dressed and walked into the kitchen. Sarah's prediction had been right: the men started to come in soon after. Sarah and Linda had prepared the night before, and it was an easy matter to feed them all. Adrian was pestered with good natured ribbing and questions while he ate. Finally, after he had finished off a large platter of bacon, eggs, and cornbread muffins, he laid his fork down and began telling the story of his encounter with Rex.

As he began, he found himself falling into a natural storyteller's rhythm, and everyone listened with acute attention. He watched the expressions on their faces and worked the story. He slowly built tension as he went along, enjoying storytelling for the first time. As he went on, Adrian realized that not only was he actually good at this, but that storytelling could be an invaluable tool in the future. When he got to the part where Rex had him at his mercy and was describing how he planned to take his revenge on Adrian, he knew he had his audience in the palm of his hand. Linda and Sarah had turned pale and looked nauseous. While he felt bad for them, it was still a good feeling, knowing that his natural shyness could be controlled. The men looked grimmer and grimmer as the story developed.

At the end, there was a general expulsion of vehement swearing at what a monster Rex had been. Given the nature of the story, Sarah didn't say anything to the men about their language in her kitchen; she felt the same way.

Adrian was in reasonably good condition again by the end of the next day. He walked the village with Linda, Scott, and Bear. They were greeted happily wherever they stopped to visit, answering numerous questions, shaking hands, and being backslapped. After they had pretty well covered the village, Adrian said, "Linda, I'm going to visit the families of the men that were killed, and then I'm going to visit the men that were injured. It would be an honor to me, and to them, if you would accompany me. It's going to be a sad and difficult thing, but it's only right to do it. Will you come?"

Linda said, "Of course. I've been visiting them already, as has most everyone else in the village. You know we already held the funeral—one large funeral burying the men in a specially chosen memorial plot. It's not Arlington National Cemetery, but it's as close as we can get to it. There will be a monument; one of the newer village men is a stone worker and is working on it now. It'll be beautiful. But it will mean something special when you visit them. Of course I'd be proud to be with you."

Over the next three days, Adrian and Linda visited with every family, spending several hours with each. Adrian didn't want it to be a quick in and out. He hugged and held each of the crying widows and children. He spent hours with each as they honored their fallen loved one by telling stories of their lives. It was one of the hardest things he had ever done, but he did it well and he did it with all of his heart. Linda's love for Adrian deepened with each passing hour as she watched him showing this gentle and caring side. She often reflected on how lucky Alice had been to have shared her life with him. Linda had had no idea of the depth of his feelings, no inkling that his heart could be that big, or that he had that much gentleness in him. He had been so rough and self-contained during the short time she had known him, but then, she had only known him during a war when he was under tremendous stress and responsibility. As she watched his heart break over and over, she was awed at this side of him that she had never suspected existed. If she had been in love with him before, she was completely lost now.

The night he completed visiting with the fallen men's families, he called his Army buddies together. They left the village and walked out into the woods where they wouldn't be bothered. Adrian carried a backpack that Sarah and Roman had prepared for him. It was filled mostly with whisky bottles, but also some sandwiches and water. They built a large fire and began drinking heavily. They told stories about Clif, each one adding details from their many missions and barroom brawls. They laughed often; silences were rare. As they got drunker, they began to sing songs and make toasts to their fallen brother. As the night wore on, they drank more and more, until they were so drunk that they couldn't stand up. This night was not only a paean to their beloved friend, but also an emotional release after the battle and a reaffirmation of their bonds. By morning, the fire had died down to ash-covered embers, and the men were passed out in various positions around it. It would be several hours before they began waking up, each with a splitting headache and nausea. This level of drinking was reserved only for occasions such as this, and the pain they would feel for the next two days was well worth enduring.

Adrian had gone through many changes since the grid had dropped. He had fallen in love, married, and settled down, then lost the first true love of his life and had wanted to die himself. He had wandered into the deep forests of the mountains to live out his life alone, and then had nearly gone insane when attacked by the cannibal raiders, and viciously killed most of them. When the cannibals had taken hostages and he'd turned to the nearby village for help, he had realized that he had at least some small talent for organizing and then leading men into war. They had won that war with no loss of life, and Adrian had come to understand just how lucky that was.

He had come home to lead men into battle again, and had won, but at a price. He had lost good men with families that would mourn their loss for the rest of their lives. He had lost Clif, his best friend. Quiet Clif was gone, and it hurt. All of these events had humbled him in ways he had never expected. Then he had started falling in love again, but at the wrong time. Too soon, he'd thought. He hadn't finished saying goodbye to Alice, and he needed more time to grieve—more time to say goodbye. He still had traveling to do, and a feeling that something is waiting on the coast. Adrian had learned the most when he was paralyzed, facing a hideous future of disconnected insanity. He had overcome that paralyzing drug to move his hand just a few inches, had channeled every ounce of his being into making that one move, and had done it. That was a lesson he believed had a purpose. There was a need for it somewhere in his future. Maybe it was a lesson for every day of the rest of his life, to understand how lucky he was to be whole, or maybe there was another, larger purpose. But now, it was time for him to go. He headed back home to prepare for the journey and say his goodbyes.

APRIL 14, EARLY MORNING

Adrian was tightening the cinch on the horse, getting ready to leave. Bear had doubled in size in the six weeks at Fort Brazos and was a yearling now, no longer needing to be carried across the saddle. Bear could run alongside now, casting about as he chose. Adrian still expected him to chase off after a rabbit someday and never come back, preferring the free life. Adrian didn't expect Bear to remain at his side until old age. Even his horse had regained its weight and vitality and seemed anxious to be going.

Adrian gave Roman and Sarah long hugs and shook hands with everyone in the village that had come to see him off. There was a lot of handshaking and backslapping, and a few hugs from some of the widowed women. There wasn't a person in the village who was able to walk who hadn't come to see him off. It was a big send-off, and Adrian was smiling hugely. "Well, looks like I have a big family!" he said, and got a cheer in return.

"Linda, would you walk with me a ways?" he asked softly. The crowd, knowing he wanted privacy and well aware by now of the feelings between them, didn't follow. Adrian took the horse's reins and Linda's hand and began walking away. When they were out of earshot, Adrian said, "I hate to leave, but I swear I have to. It's a mean thing to leave you now, and hurts me to hurt you. But please understand and believe me when I say it would be meaner to stay. Something's up in Corpus Christi. I have to go check it out. There's nothing specific; I just get the feeling that something big is up since they don't want to talk over the open air, but I need to go down there in the worst kind of way. I still owe a duty to the military, even though I was in the Army, not the Navy. If they need me for something...well, I just have to go. I feel drawn, like there's something I'm supposed to do there. Part of it comes from those strange dreams of the future I told you about. Part of it...a large part of it, honestly, is that I'm still saying goodbye to Alice."

Linda replied softly, "Adrian, you go do what you have to do. You take as much time as you need to say goodbye to her. I understand that. I'll be waiting for you. Forget what I said before—there won't be anyone else for me. Never again in this life. Two great loves is more than any woman can expect. I had one, and now...well, now I have another one, as hard as that is for me to believe. I'll be here. You just take care of yourself and come home to me as soon as you can."

Adrian gave her a long hug and a lingering kiss. It was a sad kiss, yet full of passion. Not trusting himself to say more, he mounted the horse, turned, and rode south. Linda watched him ride away. She was dry-eyed, steady of mind. She knew he would be back when his heart would let him, when his heart could allow itself to belong to her, and knowing that she could wait for him however long it took.

Adrian didn't look back. A single tear slid down his cheek. He thought, *I thought I had done hard things before, but now I know better. Nothing has ever been this hard, or felt this right.*

Adrian disappeared into the woods, the wolf running in front of him in great leaping bounds, eager to be in the woods again, the horse eagerly moving into a fast trot.

THE END

Made in the USA
Coppell, TX
12 September 2021

62233288R00135